# "Do you have any idea how much I want you?"

She lifted his hand to her mouth and kissed it. "How much?"

He chuckled. "Enough to wish this was a van instead of a sports car." Jordan turned in the seat and cupped Amanda's chin in his hand. "You're sure you're ready for this?" he asked gently.

Amanda nodded. "I'm sure. How about you?"

Jordan grinned. "I've been ready since I turned around and saw you standing in line behind me."

"You have not."

"Okay," he admitted. "It started after that, when you threw five bucks on the table to pay for your Chinese food. For just a moment, when you thought I was going to refuse it, you had blue fire in your eyes. And I had this fantasy about the whole mall being deserted—except for us, of course. I made love to you right there on the table."

Amanda felt a hot shiver go through her. "Jordan!"

# LINDA LAEL MILLER

## *Daring Moves*

**MIRA BOOKS**

**MIRA**

ISBN 1-55166-098-9

DARING MOVES

Copyright © 1990 by Linda Lael Miller.

**Printed in U.S.A.**

For Melba.
Your friendship was a gift from H.P.

# 1

The line of people waiting for an autograph reached from the bookstore down the length of the mall to the specialty luggage shop. With a sigh, Amanda Scott bought a cup of coffee from a nearby French bakery, bravely forgoing the delicate, flaky pastries inside the glass counter, and took her place behind a man in an expensive tweed overcoat.

Distractedly he turned and glanced at her, as though somehow finding her to blame for the delay. Then he pushed up his sleeve and consulted a slim gold watch. He was a couple of inches taller than Amanda, with brown hair that was only slightly too long and hazel eyes flecked with green, and he needed a shave.

Never one to pass the time in silence if an excuse to chat presented itself, Amanda took a steadying sip of her coffee and announced, "I'm buying Dr. Marshall's book for my sister, Eunice. She's going through a nasty divorce." The runaway bestseller was called *Gathering Up the*

*Pieces*, and it was meant for people who had suffered some personal loss or setback.

The stranger turned to look back at her. The pleasantly mingled scents of new snow and English Leather seemed to surround him. "Are you talking to me?" he inquired, drawing his brows together in puzzlement.

Amanda fortified herself with another sip of coffee. She hadn't meant to flirt; it was just that waiting could be so tedious. "Actually, I was," she admitted.

He surprised her with a brief but brilliant smile that practically set her back on the heels of her snow boots. In the next second his expression turned grave, but he extended a gloved hand.

"Jordan Richards," he said formally.

Gulping down the mouthful of coffee she'd just taken, Amanda returned the gesture. "Amanda Scott," she managed. "I don't usually strike up conversations with strange men in shopping malls, you understand. It's just that I was bored."

Again that blinding grin, as bright as sunlight on water.

"I see," said Jordan Richards.

The line moved a little, and they both stepped forward. Amanda suddenly felt shy, and wished she hadn't gotten off the bus at the mall. Maybe she should have gone straight home to her cozy apartment and her cat.

She reminded herself that Eunice would benefit by reading the book and that, with this purchase, her Christmas shopping would be finished. After today she could hide in her work, like a soldier crouching in a foxhole, until the holidays and all their painful associations were past.

"Too bad about Eunice," Jordan Richards remarked.

"I'll give her your condolences," Amanda promised, a smile lighting her aquamarine eyes.

The line advanced, and so did Amanda and Jordan.

"Good," he said.

Amanda finished her coffee, crumpled the cup and tossed it into a nearby trash bin. Beside the bin there was a sign that read Is Therapy For You? Attend A Free Minisession With Dr. Marshall After The Book Signing. Beneath was a diagram of the mall, with the public auditorium colored in.

"So," she ventured, "are you buying *Gathering Up the Pieces* for yourself or somebody else?"

"I'm sending it to my grandmother," Jordan answered, consulting his watch again.

Amanda wondered if he had to be somewhere else later, or if he was just an impatient person.

"What happened to her?" she asked sympathetically.

Jordan looked reluctant, but after a few moments and another step forward as the line progressed, he said, "She had some pretty heavy-duty surgery a while back."

"Oh," Amanda said, and without thinking, she reached out and patted his arm so as not to let the mention of the unknown grandmother's misfortune pass without some response from her.

Something softened in Jordan Richards's manner at the small demonstration. "Are you attending the 'free minisession'?" he asked, gesturing toward the sign. The expression in his eyes said he fully expected her to answer no.

Amanda smiled and lifted one shoulder in a shrug. "Why not? I've got the rest of the afternoon to blow, and I could learn something."

Jordan looked thoughtful. "I suppose nobody has to talk if they don't want to."

"Of course not," Amanda replied confidently, even though she had no idea what would be required. Some of the self-help groups could get pretty wild; she'd heard of people walking across burning coals in their bare feet, or letting themselves be dunked in hot tubs.

"I'll go if you'll sit beside me," Jordan said.

Amanda considered the suggestion only briefly. The mall was a well-lit place, crowded with Christmas shoppers. If Jordan Richards were some kind of weirdo—and that seemed unlikely, unless crackpots were dressing like models in *Gentlemen's Quarterly* these days—she would be perfectly safe. "Okay," she said with another shrug.

After the decision was made, they lapsed into a companionable silence. Nearly fifteen minutes had passed by the time Jordan reached the author's table.

Dr. Eugene Marshall, the famous psychology guru, signed his name in a confident scrawl and handed Jordan a book. Amanda had her volume autographed and followed her new acquaintance to the cash register.

Once they'd both paid, they left the store together.

There was already a mob gathered at the double doors of the mall's community auditorium, and according to a sign on an easel, the minisession would start in another ten minutes.

Jordan glanced at the line of fast-food places across the concourse. "Would you like some coffee or something?"

Amanda shook her head, then reached up to pull her light, shoulder-length hair from under the collar of her coat. "No, thanks. What kind of work do you do, Mr. Richards?"

"'Jordan,'" he corrected. He took off his overcoat and draped it over one arm, then loosened his tie and collar slightly. "What kind of work do you think I do?"

Amanda assessed him, narrowing her blue eyes. Jordan looked fit, and he even had a bit of a suntan, but she doubted he worked with his hands. His clothes marked him as an upper-management type, and so did that gold watch he kept checking. "You're a stockbroker," she guessed.

He chuckled. "Close. I'm a partner in an investment firm. What do you do?"

People were starting to move into the auditorium and take seats, and Amanda and Jordan moved along with them. With a half smile, she answered, "Guess."

He considered her thoughtfully. "You're a flight attendant for a major airline," he decided after several moments had passed.

Amanda took his conjecture as a compliment, even though it was wrong. "I'm the assistant manager of the Evergreen Hotel." They found seats near the middle of the auditorium, and Jordan took the one on the aisle. Amanda was just daring to hope she was making a favorable impression, when her stomach rumbled.

"And you haven't had lunch yet," Jordan stated with another of those lethal, quicksilver grins. "It just so happens that I'm a little hungry myself. How about something from that Chinese fast-food place I saw out there—after we're done with the minisession, I mean?"

Again Amanda smiled. She seemed to be smiling a lot, which was odd, because she hadn't felt truly happy since before James Brockman had swept into her life, turned it upside down and swept out again. "I'd like that," she heard herself say.

Just then Dr. Marshall walked out onto the auditorium stage. At his appearance, Jordan became noticeably uncomfortable, shifting in his seat and drawing one Italian-leather-shod foot up to rest on the opposite knee.

The famous author introduced himself, just in case someone who had never watched a TV talk show might have wandered in, and announced that he wanted the audience to break up into groups of twelve.

Jordan looked even more discomfited, and probably wouldn't have participated if a group hadn't formed around him and Amanda. To make things even more interesting, at least to Amanda's way of thinking, the handsome, silver-haired Dr. Marshall chose their group to work with, while his assistants took the others.

"All right, people," he began in a tone of pleasant authority, "let's get started." His knowing gray eyes swept the small gathering. "Why does everybody look so worried? This will be relatively painless—all we're going to do is talk about ourselves a little." He looked at Amanda.

"What's your name?" he asked directly. "And what's the worst thing that's happened to you in the past year?"

She swallowed. "Amanda Scott. And—the worst thing?"

Dr. Marshall nodded with kindly amusement.

All of the sudden Amanda wished she'd gone to a matinee or stayed home to clean her apartment. She didn't want to talk about James, especially not in front of strangers, but she was basically an honest person and *James* was the worst thing that had happened to her in a very long time. Not looking at Jordan, she answered, "I fell in love with a man and he turned out to be married."

"What did you do when you found out?" the doctor asked reasonably.

"I cried a lot," Amanda answered, forgetting for the moment that there were twelve other people listening in, including Jordan.

"Did you break off the relationship?" Dr. Marshall pressed.

Amanda still felt the pain and humiliation she'd known when James's wife had stormed into her office and made a scene. Before that, Amanda hadn't even suspected the terrible truth. "Yes," she replied softly with a miserable nod.

"Is this experience still affecting your life?"

Amanda wished she dared to glance at Jordan to see how he was reacting, but she didn't have the courage. She lowered her eyes. "I guess it is."

"Did you stop trusting men?"

Considering all the dates she'd refused in the months since she'd disentangled herself from James, Amanda supposed she had stopped trusting men. Even worse, she'd stopped trusting her own instincts. "Yes," she answered very softly.

Dr. Marshall reached out to touch her shoulder. "I'm not going to pretend you can solve your problems just by sitting in on a minisession, or even by reading my book, but I think it's time for you to stop hiding and take some risks. Agreed?"

Amanda was surprised at the man's insight. "Agreed," she said, and right then and there she made up her mind to read Eunice's copy of *Gathering Up the Pieces* before she wrapped it.

The doctor's attention shifted to the man sitting on Amanda's left. He said he'd lost his job, and the fact that Christmas was coming up made things harder. A woman in the row behind Amanda talked about her child's serious illness. Finally, after about twenty minutes had passed, everyone had spoken except Jordan.

He rubbed his chin, which was already showing a five o'clock shadow, and cleared his throat. Amanda, feeling his tension and reluctance as though they were her own, laid her hand gently on his arm.

"The worst thing that ever happened to me," he said in a low, almost inaudible voice, "was losing my wife."

"How did it happen?" the doctor asked.

Jordan looked as though he wanted to bolt out of his chair and stride up the aisle to the doors, but he answered the question. "A motorcycle accident."

"Were you driving?" Dr. Marshall's expression was sympathetic.

"Yes," Jordan replied after a long silence.

"And you're still not ready to talk about it," the doctor deduced.

"That's right," Jordan said. And he got up and walked slowly up the aisle and out of the auditorium.

Amanda followed, catching up just outside. She didn't quite dare to touch his arm again, yet he slowed down at the sound of her footsteps. "How about that Chinese food you promised me?" she asked gently.

Jordan met her eyes, and for just a moment, she saw straight through to his soul. What pain he'd suffered.

"Sure," he replied, and his voice was hoarse.

"I'm all through with my Christmas shopping," Amanda announced once they were seated at a table, Number Three Regulars in front of them from the Chinese fast-food place. "How about you?"

"My secretary does mine," Jordan responded. He looked relieved at her choice of topic.

"That's above and beyond the call of duty," Amanda remarked lightly. "I hope you're giving her something terrific."

Jordan smiled at that. "She gets a sizable bonus."

"Good."

It was obvious Jordan was feeling better. His eyes twinkled, and some of the strain had left his face.

"I'm glad company policy meets with your approval."

It was surprising, considering her unfortunate and all-too-recent experiences with James, but it wasn't until that moment that Amanda realized that she hadn't checked Jordan's hand for a wedding band. She glanced at the appropriate finger, even though she knew it would be bare, and saw a white strip where the ring had been.

"Like I said, I'm a widower," he told her with a slight smile, obviously having read her glance accurately.

"I'm sorry," Amanda told him.

He speared a piece of sweet-and-sour chicken. "It's been three years."

It seemed to Amanda that the white space on his ring finger should have filled in after three years. "That's quite a while," she said, wondering if she should just get up from her chair, collect her book and her coat and leave. In the end she didn't, because a glance at her watch told her it was still forty minutes until the next bus left. Besides, she was hungry.

Jordan sighed. "Sometimes it seems like three centuries."

Amanda bit her lower lip, then burst out, "You aren't one of those creeps who goes around saying he doesn't have a wife when he really does, are you? I mean, you could have remarried."

He looked very tired all of a sudden, and pale beneath his tan. Amanda wondered why he hadn't gotten around to shaving.

"No," he said. "I'm not married."

Amanda dropped her eyes to her food, ashamed that she'd asked the question, even though she wouldn't have taken it back. The experience with James had taught her that a woman couldn't be too careful about such things.

"Amanda?"

She lifted her gaze to see him studying her. "What?"

"What was his name?"

"What was whose name?"

"The guy who told you he wasn't married."

Amanda cleared her throat and shifted nervously in her chair. The thought of James didn't cause her pain anymore, but she didn't know Jordan Richards well enough to tell him just how badly she'd been hoodwinked. A sudden, crazy panic seized her. "Gosh, look at the time," she said, pulling back her sleeve to check her watch a split second after she'd spoken. "I'd better get home." She bolted out of her chair and put her coat back on, then reached for her purse and the bag from the bookstore. She laid a five-dollar bill on the table to pay for her dinner. "It was nice meeting you."

Jordan frowned and slowly pushed back his chair, then stood. "Wait a minute, Amanda. You're not playing fair."

He was right. Jordan hadn't run away, however much he had probably wanted to, and she wouldn't, either.

She sank back into her seat, all too aware that people at surrounding tables were looking on with interest.

"You're not ready to talk about him," Jordan said, sitting down again, "and I'm not ready to talk about her. Deal?"

"Deal," Amanda said.

They discussed the Seattle Seahawks after that, and the Chinese artifacts on display at one of the museums. Then Jordan walked with her to the nearest corner and waited until the bus pulled up.

"Goodbye, Amanda," he said as she climbed the steps.

She dropped her change into the slot and smiled over one shoulder. "Thanks for the company."

He waved as the bus pulled away, and Amanda ached with a bittersweet loneliness she'd never known before, not even in the awful days after her breakup with James.

When Amanda arrived at her apartment building on Seattle's Queen Anne Hill, she was still thinking about Jordan. He'd wanted to offer to drive her home, she knew, but he'd had the good grace not to, and Amanda liked him for that.

In her mailbox she found a sheaf of bills waiting for her. "I'll never save enough to start a bed and breakfast at this rate," she complained to her black-and-white long-haired cat, Gershwin, when he met her at the door.

Gershwin was unsympathetic. As usual, he was interested only in his dinner.

After flipping on the lights, dropping her purse and the book onto the hall table and hanging her coat on the brass-plated tree that was really too large for that little space, Amanda went into the kitchenette.

Gershwin purred and wound himself around her ankles as she opened a can of cat food, but when she scraped it out onto his dish, he abandoned her without compunction.

While Gershwin gobbled, Amanda went back to the mail she'd picked up in the lobby and flipped through it again. Three bills, a you-may-have-already-won and a letter from Eunice.

Amanda set the other envelopes down and opened the crisp blue one with her sister's return address printed in italics in one corner. She was disappointed when she realized that the letter was just another litany of Eunice's soon-to-be-ex-husband's sins, and she set it aside to finish later.

In the bathroom she started water running into her huge claw-footed tub, then stripped off the skirt and sweater she'd worn to the mall. After disposing of her underthings and panty hose, Amanda climbed into the soothing water.

Gershwin pushed the door open in that officious way cats have and bounded up to stand on the tub's edge with perfect balance. Like a tight-rope walker, he strolled back and forth along the chipped porcelain, telling Amanda about his day in a series of companionable meows.

Amanda listened politely as she bathed, but her mind was wandering. She was thinking about Jordan Richards and that recently removed wedding band of his.

She sighed. All her instincts told her he was telling the truth about his marital status, but those same instincts had once insisted that James was all right, too.

Amanda was waiting when the bus pulled up at her corner the next morning. The weather was a little warmer, and the snow, so unusual in Seattle, was already melting.

Fifteen minutes later Amanda walked through the huge revolving door of the Evergreen Hotel. Its lush Oriental carpets were soft beneath the soles of her shoes, and crystal chandeliers winked overhead, their multicolored reflections blazing in the floor-to-ceiling mirrors.

Amanda took the elevator to the third floor, where the hotel's business offices were. As she was passing through the small reception area, Mindy Simmons hailed her from her desk.

"Mr. Mansfield is sick today," she said in an undertone. Mindy was small and pretty, with long brown hair and expressive green eyes. "Your desk is buried in messages."

Amanda went into her office and started dealing with problems. The plumbing in the presidential suite was on the fritz, so she called to make sure Maintenance was on top of the situation. A Mrs. Edman in 1203 suspected one of the maids of stealing her pearl earring, and someone had mixed up some dates at the reception desk—two couples were expecting to occupy the bridal suite on the same night.

It was noon when Amanda finished straightening everything out—Mrs. Edman's pearl earring had fallen behind the television set, the plumbing in the presidential suite was back in working order and each of the newlywed couples would have rooms to themselves. At Mindy's suggestion, she and Amanda went to the busy Westlake Mall for lunch, buying salads at one of the fast-food restaurants and taking a table near a window.

"Two more weeks and I start my vacation," Mindy stated enthusiastically, pouring dressing from a little carton over her salad. "Christmas at Big Mountain. I can hardly wait."

Amanda would just as soon have skipped Christmas altogether if she could have gotten the rest of the world to go along with the idea, but of course she didn't say that. "You and Pete will have a great time at the ski resort."

Mindy was chewing, and she swallowed before answering. "It's just great of his parents to take us along—we could never have afforded it on our own."

With a nod, Amanda poked her fork into a cherry tomato.

"What are you doing over the holidays?" Mindy asked.

Amanda forced a smile. "I'm going to be working," she reminded her friend.

"I know that, but what about a tree and presents and a turkey?"

"I'll have all those things at my mom and stepdad's place."

Mindy, who knew about James and all the dashed hopes he'd left in his wake, looked sympathetic. "You need to meet a new man."

Amanda bristled a little. "It just so happens that a woman can have a perfectly happy life without a man hanging around."

Mindy looked doubtful. "Sure," she said.

"Besides, I met someone just yesterday."

"Who?"

Amanda concentrated on her salad for several long moments. "His name is Jordan Richards, and—"

"Jordan Richards?" Mindy interrupted excitedly. "Wow! How did you ever manage to meet him?"

A little insulted that Mindy seemed to think Jordan was so far out of her orbit that even meeting him was a feat to get excited about, Amanda frowned. "We were in line together at a bookstore. Do you know him?"

"Not exactly," Mindy admitted, subsiding a little. "But my father-in-law does. Jordan Richards practically doubled his retirement fund for him, and they're always writing about him in the financial section of the Sunday paper."

"I didn't know you read that section," Amanda remarked.

"I don't," Mindy admitted readily, unwrapping a bread stick. "But we have dinner with my in-laws practically every Sunday, and that's all Pete and his dad ever talk about. Did he ask you out?"

"Who?"

"Jordan Richards, silly."

Amanda shook her head. "No, we just had Chinese food together and talked a little." She deliberately left out the part about how they'd gone to the minitherapy session and the way she'd reacted when Jordan had asked her about James.

Mindy looked disappointed. "Well, he did ask for your number, didn't he?"

"No. But he knows where I work. If he wants to call, I suppose he will."

A delighted smile lit Mindy's face. Positive thinking was an art form with her. "He'll call. I just know it."

Amanda grinned. "If he does, I won't be able to accept the glory—I owe it all to an article I read in *Cosmo*. I think it was called 'Big Girls Should Talk to Strangers,' or something like that."

Mindy lifted her diet cola in a rousing roast. "Here's to Jordan Richards and a red-hot romance!"

With a chuckle, Amanda touched her cup to Mindy's and drank a toast to something that would probably never happen.

Back at the hotel more crises were waiting to be solved, and there was a message on Amanda's desk, scrawled by the typist who'd filled in for Mindy during lunch. Jordan Richards had called.

A peculiar tightness constricted Amanda's throat, and a flutter started in the pit of her stomach. Mindy's toast echoed in her ears: *"Here's to Jordan Richards and a red-hot romance."*

Amanda laid down the message, telling herself she didn't have time to return the call, then picked it up again. Before she knew it, her finger was punching out the numbers.

"Striner, Striner and Richards," sang a receptionist's voice at the other end of the line.

Amanda drew a deep breath, squared her shoulders and exhaled. "This is Amanda Scott," she said in her most professional voice. "I'm returning a call from Jordan Richards."

"One moment, please."

After a series of clicks and buzzes another female voice came on the line. "Jordan Richards's office. May I help you?"

Again Amanda gave her name. And again she was careful to say she was returning a call that had originated with Jordan.

There was another buzz, then Jordan's deep, crisp voice saying, "Richards."

Amanda hadn't expected a simple thing like the man saying his name to affect her the way it did. It was the strangest sensation to feel dizzy over something like that. She dropped into the swivel chair behind her desk. "Hi. It's Amanda."

"Amanda."

Coming from him, her own name had the same strange impact as his had had.

"How are you?" he asked.

Amanda swallowed. She was a professional with a very responsible job. It was ridiculous to be overwhelmed by something so simple and ordinary as the timbre of a man's voice. "I'm fine," she answered. Nothing more imaginative came to her, and she sat there behind her broad desk, blushing like an eighth-grade schoolgirl trying to work up the courage to ask a boy to a sock hop.

His low, masculine chuckle came over the wire to surround her like a mystical caress. "If I promise not to ask any more questions about you know who, will you go out with me? Some friends of mine are having an informal dinner tonight on their houseboat."

Amanda still felt foolish for talking about James in the therapy session, then practically bolting when Jordan brought him up again over Chinese food. Lately she just seemed to be a mass of contradictions, feeling one way one minute, another the next. What it all came down to was the fact that Dr. Marshall was right—she needed to start taking chances again. "Sounds like fun," she said after drawing a deep breath.

"Pick you up at seven?"

"Yes." And she gave him her address. A little thrill went through her as she laid the receiver back on its cradle, but there was no more time to think about Jordan. The telephone immediately rang again.

"Amanda Scott."

The chef's assistant was calling. A pipe had broken, and the kitchen was flooding fast.

"Just another manic day," Amanda muttered as she hurried off to investigate.

# 2

It was ten minutes after six when Amanda got off the bus in front of her apartment building and dashed inside. After collecting her mail, she hurried up the stairs and jammed her key into the lock. Jordan was picking her up in less than an hour, and she had a hundred things to do to get ready.

Since he'd told her the evening would be a casual one, she selected gray woolen slacks and a cobalt-blue blouse. After a hasty shower, she put on fresh makeup and quickly wove her hair into a French braid.

Gershwin stood on the back of the toilet the whole time she was getting ready, lamenting the treatment of house cats in contemporary America. She had just given him his dinner when a knock sounded at the door.

Amanda's heart lurched like a dizzy ballet dancer, and she wondered why she was being such a ninny. Jordan Richards was just a man, nothing more. And so what if he was successful? She met a lot of men like him in her line of work.

She opened the door and knew a moment of pure exaltation at the look of approval in Jordan's eyes.

"Hi," he said. He wore jeans and a sport shirt, and his hands rested comfortably in the pockets of his brown leather jacket. "You look fantastic."

Amanda thought he looked pretty fantastic himself, but she didn't say so because she'd used up that week's quota of bold moves by talking about James in front of people she didn't know. "Thanks," she said, stepping back to admit him.

Gershwin did a couple of turns around Jordan's ankles and meowed his approval. With a chuckle, Jordan bent to pick him up. "Look at the size of this guy. Is he on steroids or what?"

Amanda laughed. "No, but I suspect him of throwing wild parties and sending out for pizza when I'm not around."

After scratching the cat once behind the ears, Jordan set him down again with a chuckle, but his eyes were serious when he looked at Amanda.

Something in his expression made her breasts grow heavy and her nipples tighten beneath the smooth silk of her blouse. "I suppose we'd better go," she said, sounding somewhat lame even to her own ears.

"Right," Jordan agreed. His voice had the same effect on Amanda it had had earlier. She felt the starch go out of her knees and she was breathless, as though she'd accidentally stepped onto a runaway skateboard.

She took her blue cloth coat from the coat tree, and Jordan helped her into it. She felt his fingertips brush her nape as he lifted her braid from beneath the collar, and hoped he didn't notice that she trembled ever so slightly at his touch.

His car, a sleek black Porsche—Amanda decided then and there that he didn't have kids of his own—was parked at the curb. Jordan opened the passenger door and walked around to get behind the wheel after Amanda was settled.

Soon they were streaking toward Lake Union. It was only when he switched on the windshield wipers that Amanda realized it was raining.

"Have you lived in Seattle long?" she asked, uncomfortable with a silence Jordan hadn't seemed to mind.

"I live on Vashon Island now—I've been somewhere in the vicinity all my life," he answered. "What about you?"

"Seattle's home," Amanda replied.

"Have you ever wanted to live anywhere else?"

She smiled. "Sure. Paris, London, Rome. But after I graduated from college, I was hired to work at the Evergreen, so I settled down here."

"You know what they say—life is what happens while we're making other plans. I always intended to work on Wall Street myself."

"Do you regret staying here?"

Amanda had expected a quick, light denial. Instead she received a sober glance and a low, "Sometimes, yes. Things might have been very different if I'd gone to New York."

For some reason Amanda's gaze was drawn to the pale line across Jordan's left-hand ring finger. Although the windows were closed and the heater was going, Amanda suppressed a shiver. She didn't say anything until Lake Union, with its diamondlike trim of lit houseboats, came into sight. Since the holidays were approaching, the place was even more of a spectacle than usual.

"It looks like a tangle of Christmas tree lights."

Jordan surprised her with one of his fleeting, devastating grins.

"You have a colorful way of putting things, Amanda Scott."

She smiled. "Do your friends like living on a houseboat?"

"I think so," he answered, "but they're planning to move in the spring. They're expecting a baby."

Although lots of children were growing up on Lake Union, Amanda could understand why Jordan's friends would want to bring their little one up on dry land. Her thoughts turned bittersweet as she wondered whether she would ever have a child of her own. She was already twenty-eight—time was running out.

As he pulled the car into a parking lot near the wharves and shut the engine off, she sat up a little straighter, realizing that she'd left his remark dangling. "I'm sorry...I...how nice for them that they're having a baby."

Unexpectedly Jordan reached out and closed his hand over Amanda's. "Did I say something wrong?" he asked with a gentleness that almost brought tears to her eyes.

Amanda shook her head. "Of course not. Let's go in—I'm anxious to meet your friends."

David and Claudia Chamberlin were an attractive couple in their early thirties, he with dark hair and eyes, she with very fair coloring and green eyes. They were both architects, and framed drawings and photographs of their work graced the walls of the small but elegantly furnished houseboat.

Amanda thought of her own humble apartment with Gershwin as its outstanding feature, and wondered if Jordan thought she was dull.

Claudia seemed genuinely interested in her, though, and her greeting was warm. "It's good to see Jordan back in circulation—finally," she confided in a whisper when she and Amanda were alone beside the table where an array of wonderful food was being set out by the caterer's helpers.

Amanda didn't reply to the comment right away, but her gaze strayed to Jordan, who was standing only a few feet away, talking with David. "I guess it's been pretty hard for him," she ventured, pretending to know more than she did.

"The worst," Claudia agreed. She pulled Amanda a little distance farther from the men. "We thought he'd never get over losing Becky."

Uneasily Amanda recalled the pale stripe Jordan's wedding band had left on his finger. Perhaps, she reflected warily, there was a corresponding mark on his soul.

Later, when Amanda had met everyone in the room and mingled accordingly, Jordan laid her coat gently over her shoulders. "How about going out on deck with me for a few minutes?" he asked quietly. "I need some air."

Once again Amanda felt that peculiar lurching sensation deep inside. "Sure," she said with a wary glance at the rain-beaded windows.

"The rain stopped a little while ago," Jordan assured her with a slight grin.

The way he seemed to know what she was thinking was disconcerting.

They left the main cabin through a door on the side, and because the deck was slippery, Jordan put a strong arm around Amanda's waist. She was fully independent, but she still liked the feeling of being looked after.

The lights of the harbor twinkled on the dark waters of the lake, and Jordan studied them for a while before asking, "So, what do you think of Claudia and David?"

Amanda smiled. "They're pretty interesting," she replied. "I suppose you know they were married in India when they were there with the Peace Corps."

Jordan propped an elbow on the railing and nodded. "David and Claudia are nothing if not unconventional. That's one of the reasons I like them so much."

Amanda was slightly deflated, though she tried hard not to reveal the fact. With her ordinary job, cat and apartment, she knew she must seem prosaic compared to the Chamberlins. Perhaps it was the strange sense of hopelessness she felt that made her reckless enough to ask, "What about your wife? Was she unconventional?"

He turned away from her to stare out at the water, and for a long moment she was sure he didn't intend to answer. Finally, however, he said in a low voice, "She had a degree in marine biology, but she didn't work after the kids were born."

It was the first mention he'd made of any children—Amanda had been convinced, in fact, that he had none. "Kids?" she asked in a small and puzzled voice.

Jordan looked at her in a way that was almost, but not quite, defensive. "There are two—Jessica's five and Lisa's four."

Amanda knew a peculiar joy, as though she'd stumbled upon an unexpected treasure. She couldn't help the quick, eager smile that curved her lips. "I thought—well, when you were driving a Porsche—"

He smiled back at her in an oddly somber way. "Jessie and Lisa live with my sister over in Port Townsend."

Amanda's jubilation deflated. "They live with your sister? I don't understand."

Jordan sighed. "Becky died two weeks after the accident, and I was in the hospital for close to three months. Karen—my sister—and her husband, Paul, took the kids. By the time I got back on my feet, the four of them had become a family. I couldn't see breaking it up."

An overwhelming sadness caused Amanda to grip the railing for a moment to keep from being swept away by the sheer power of the emotion.

Reading her expression, Jordan gently touched the tip of her nose. "Ready to call it a night? You look tired."

Amanda nodded, too close to tears to speak. She had a tendency to empathize with other people's joys and sorrows, and she was momentarily crushed by the weight of what Jordan had been through.

"I see my daughters often," he assured her, tenderness glinting in his eyes. He kissed her lightly on the mouth, then took her elbow and escorted her back inside the cabin.

They said their goodbyes to David and Claudia Chamberlin, then walked up the wharf to Jordan's car. He was a perfect gentleman, opening the door for Amanda, and she settled wearily into the suede passenger seat.

Back at Amanda's building, Jordan again helped her out of the car, and he walked her to her door. Amanda waited until the last possible second to decide whether she was going to invite him in, breaking her own suspense by blurting out, "Would you like a cup of coffee or something?"

Jordan's hazel eyes twinkled as he placed one hand on either side of the doorjamb, effectively trapping Amanda between his arms. "Not tonight," he said softly.

Amanda's blue eyes widened in confusion. "Don't look now," she replied in a burst of daring cowardice, "but you're sending out conflicting messages."

He chuckled, and his lips touched hers, very tenderly.

Amanda felt a jolt of spiritual electricity spark through her system, burning away every memory of James's touch. Surprise made her draw back from Jordan so suddenly that her head bumped hard against the door.

Jordan lowered one hand to caress her crown, and she felt the French braid coming undone beneath his fingers.

"Careful," he murmured, and then he kissed her again.

This time there was hunger in his touch, and a sweet, frightening power that made Amanda's knees unsteady.

She laid her hands lightly on his chest, trying to ground this second mystical shock, but he interpreted the contact differently and drew back.

"Good night, Amanda," he said quietly. He waited until she'd unlocked her door with a trembling hand, and then he walked away.

Inside the apartment Amanda flipped on the living room light, crossed to the sofa and sagged onto it. She felt as though she were leaning over the edge of a great canyon and the rocks were slipping away beneath her feet.

Gershwin hurled himself into her lap with a loud meow, and she ran one hand distractedly along his silky back. Dr. Marshall had said it was time she started taking chances, and she had an awful feeling she was on the brink of the biggest risk of her life.

The massive redwood-and-glass house overlooking Puget Sound was dark and unwelcoming that night when Jordan pulled into the driveway and reached for the small remote control device lying on his dashboard. He'd barely made the last ferry to the island, and he was tired.

As the garage door rolled upward, he thought of Amanda, and shifted uncomfortably on the seat. He would have given half his stock portfolio to have her sitting beside him now, to talk with her over coffee in the kitchen or wine in front of the fireplace . . .

To take her to his bed.

Jordan got out of the car and slammed the door behind him. The garage was dark, but he didn't flip on a light until he reached the kitchen. Becky had always said he had the night vision of a vampire.

Becky. He clung to the memory of her smile, her laughter, her perfume. She'd been tiny and spirited, with dark hair and eyes, and it seemed to Jordan that she'd never been far from his side, even after her death. He'd loved her to an excruciating degree, but for the past few months she'd been steadily receding from his mind and heart. Now, with the coming of Amanda, her image seemed to be growing more indistinct with every passing moment.

Jordan glanced into the laundry room, needing something real and mundane to focus on. A pile of jeans, sweatshirts and towels lay on the floor, so he crammed as much as he could into the washing machine, then added soap and turned the dial. A comforting, ordinary sound resulted.

Returning to the kitchen, Jordan shrugged out of his leather jacket and laid it over one of the bar stools at the counter. He opened the refrigerator, studied its contents without actually focusing on a single item, then closed it again. He wasn't hungry for anything except Amanda, and it was too soon for that.

Too soon, he reflected with a rueful grin as he walked through the dining room to the front entryway and the stairs. He hadn't bothered with such niceties as timing with the women he'd dated over the past two years—in truth, their feelings just hadn't mattered much to him, though he'd never been deliberately unkind.

He trailed his hand over the top of the polished oak banister as he climbed the stairs. With Amanda, things were different. Timing was crucial, and so were her feelings.

The empty house yawned around Jordan as he opened his bedroom door and went inside. In the adjoining bathroom he took off his clothes and dropped them neatly into the hamper, then stepped into the shower.

Thinking of Amanda again, he turned on the cold water and endured its biting chill until some of the intolerable heat had abated. But while he was brushing his teeth, Amanda sneaked back into his mind.

He saw her standing on the deck of the Chamberlins' boat, looking up at him with that curious vulnerability showing in her blue-green eyes. It was as though she didn't know how beautiful she was, or how strong, and yet she had to, because she was out there making a life for herself.

Rubbing his now-stubbled chin, Jordan wandered into the bedroom, threw back the covers and slid between the sheets. He felt the first stirrings of rage as he thought about the mysterious James and the damage he'd done to Amanda's soul. Jordan had seen the bruises in her eyes every time she'd looked at him, and the memory made him want to find the bastard who'd hurt her and systematically tear him apart.

Jordan turned onto his stomach and tried to put the scattered images of the past two days out of his thoughts. This time, just before he dropped off to sleep, was reserved for thoughts of Becky, as always.

He waited, but his late wife's face didn't form in his mind. He could only see Amanda, with her wide, trusting blue eyes, her soft, spun-honey hair, her shapely and inviting body. He wanted her with a desperation that made his loins ache.

Furious, Jordan slammed one fist into the mattress and flipped onto his back, training all his considerable energy on remembering Becky's face.

He couldn't.

After several minutes of concentrated effort, all of it fruitless, panic seized him, and he bolted upright, switched on the lamp and reached for the picture on his nightstand.

Becky smiled back at him from the photograph as if to say, *Don't worry, sweetheart. Everything will be okay.*

With a raspy sigh, Jordan set the picture back on the table and turned out the light. Becky's favorite reassurance didn't work that night. Maybe things would be okay in the long run, but there was a lot of emotional white water between him and any kind of happy ending.

It was Saturday morning, and Amanda luxuriated in the fact that she didn't have to put on makeup, style her hair, or even get dressed if she didn't want to. She really tried to be lazy, but she felt strangely ambitious, and there was no getting around it.

She climbed out of bed and padded barefoot into the kitchen, where she got the coffee maker going and fed Gershwin. Then she had a quick shower and dressed in battered jeans, a Seahawks T-shirt and sneakers.

She was industriously vacuuming the living room rug, when the telephone rang.

The sound was certainly nothing unusual, but it fairly stopped Amanda's heart. She kicked the switch on the vacuum cleaner with her toe and lunged for the telephone, hoping to hear Jordan's voice since she hadn't seen or heard from him in nearly a week.

Instead it was her mother. "Hello, darling," said Marion Whitfield. "You sound breathless. Were you just coming in from the store or something?"

Amanda sank onto the couch. "No, I was only doing housework," she replied, feeling deflated even though she loved and admired this woman who had made a life for herself and both her daughters after the man of the house had walked out on them all.

"That's nice," Marion commented, for she was a great believer in positive reinforcement. "Listen, I called to ask if you'd like to go Christmas shopping with me. We could have lunch, too, and maybe even take in a movie."

Amanda sighed. She still didn't feel great about Christmas, and the stores and restaurants would be jam-packed. The theaters, of course, would be full of screaming children left there by harried mothers trying to complete their shopping. "I think I'll just stay home, if you don't mind." She stated the refusal in a kindly tone, not wanting to hurt her mother's feelings.

"Is everything all right?"

Amanda caught one fingernail between her teeth for a moment before answering, "Mostly, yes."

"It's time you put that nasty experience with James Brockman behind you," Marion said forthrightly.

The two women were friends, as well as mother and daughter, and Amanda was not normally secretive with Marion. However, the thing with Jordan was too new and too fragile to be discussed; after all, he might never call again. "I'm trying, Mom," she replied.

"Well, Bob and I want you to come over for dinner soon. Like tomorrow, for instance."

"I'll let you know," Amanda promised quickly as the doorbell made its irritating buzz. "And stop worrying about me, okay?"

"Okay," Marion answered without conviction just before Amanda hung up.

Amanda expected one of the neighbor children, or maybe the postman with a package, so when she opened the door and found Jordan standing in the hallway, she felt as though she'd just run into a wall at full tilt.

For his part, Jordan looked a little bewildered, as though he might be surprised to find himself at Amanda's door. "I should have called," he said.

Amanda recovered herself. "Come in," she replied with a smile.

He hesitated for a moment, then stepped into the apartment, his hands tucked into the pockets of his jacket. He was wearing jeans and a green turtleneck, and his brown hair was damp from the Seattle drizzle. "I was wondering if you'd like to go out to lunch or something."

Amanda glanced at the clock on the mantel and was amazed to see that it was nearly noon. The morning had flown by in a flurry of housecleaning. "Sure," she said. "I'll just clean up a little—"

He reached out and caught hold of her hand when she would have disappeared into her bedroom. "You look fine," he told her, and his voice was very low, like the rumble of an earthquake deep down in the ground.

By sheer force of will, Amanda shored up her knees, only to have him pull her close and lock his hands lightly behind the small of her back. A hot flush made her cheeks ache, and she had to force herself to meet his eyes.

Jordan chuckled. "Do I really scare you so much?" he asked.

Amanda wet her lips with the tip of her tongue in an unconscious display of nervousness. "Yes."

"Why?"

The question was reasonable, but Amanda didn't know the answer. "I'm not sure."

He grinned. "Where would you like to go for lunch?"

She would have been content not to go out at all, preferring just to stand there in his arms all afternoon, breathing in his scent and enjoying the lean, hard feel of his body against hers. She gave herself an inward shake. "You know, I just refused a similar invitation from my mother, and she would have thrown in a movie."

Jordan laughed and smoothed Amanda's bangs back from her forehead. "All right, so will I."

But Amanda shook her head. "Too many munchkins screaming and throwing popcorn."

His expression changed almost imperceptibly. "Don't you like kids?"

"I love them," Amanda answered, "except when they're traveling in herds."

Jordan chuckled again and gave her another light kiss. "Okay, we'll go to something R-rated. Nobody under seventeen admitted without a parent."

"You've got a deal," Amanda replied.

Just as he was helping her get into her coat, the telephone rang. Praying there wasn't a disaster at the Evergreen to be taken care of, Amanda answered, "Hello?"

"Hello, Amanda." She hadn't heard that voice in six long months, and the sound of it stunned her. It was James.

Grimacing at Jordan, she spoke into the receiver. "I don't want to talk to you, now or ever."

"Please don't hang up," James said quickly.

Amanda bit down on her lip and lowered her eyes. "What is it?"

"Madge is divorcing me."

She drew a deep breath and let it out again. "Congratulations, James," she said, not with cruelty but with resignation. After all, it was no great surprise, and she had no idea why he felt compelled to share the news with her.

"I'd like for you and me to get back together," he said in that familiar tone that had once rendered her pliant and gullible.

"There's absolutely no chance of that," Amanda replied, forcing herself to meet Jordan's gaze again. He was standing at the door, his hand on the knob, watching her with concern but not condemnation. "Goodbye, James." With that, she placed the receiver back in its cradle.

Jordan remained where he was for a long moment, then he crossed the room to where Amanda stood, bundled in her coat, and gently lifted her hair out from under her collar. "Still want to go out?" he asked quietly.

Amanda was oddly shaken, but she nodded, and they left the apartment together. The phone began ringing again when they reached the top of the stairs, but this time Amanda made no effort to answer it.

"I guess I can't blame him for being persistent," Jordan remarked when they were seated in the Porsche. "You're a beautiful woman, Amanda."

She sighed, ignoring the compliment because it didn't register. "I'll never forgive James for lying to me the way he did," she got out. Tears stung her eyes as she remembered the blinding pain of his deceit.

Jordan pulled out into the rainy-day traffic and kept his eyes on the road. "He wants you back," he guessed.

Amanda noticed that his hands tensed slightly around the steering wheel.

"That's what he said," she confessed, staring out at the decorated streets but not really seeing them.

"Do you believe him?"

Amanda shrugged. "It doesn't matter whether I do or not. I've made my decision and I'm not going to change my mind." She found some tissue in her purse and resolutely dried her eyes, trying in vain to convince herself that Jordan hadn't noticed she was crying.

He drove to a pizza joint across the street from a mall north of the city. "This okay?" he asked, bringing the sleek car to a stop in one of the few parking spaces available. "We could order takeout if you'd rather not go in."

Amanda drew a deep breath, composing herself. The time with James was behind her, and she wanted to keep it there, to enjoy the here and now with Jordan. Christmas crowds or none. "Let's eat here," she said.

He favored her with a half grin and came around to open her door for her. As she stood, she accidentally brushed against him, and felt that familiar twisting ache deep inside herself. She was going to end up making love with Jordan Richards, she just knew it. It was inevitable.

The realization that he was reading her thoughts once more made Amanda blush, and she drew back when he took her hand. His grip only became firmer, however, and she didn't try to pull away again. She was in the mood to follow where Jordan might lead—which, to Amanda's way of thinking, made it a darned good thing they were approaching the door of a pizza parlor instead of a bedroom.

# 3

The pizza was uncommonly good, it seemed to Amanda, but memories of the R-rated movie they saw afterward made her fidget in the passenger seat of Jordan's Porsche. "I've never heard of anybody doing that with an ice cube," she remarked with a slight frown.

Jordan laughed. "That was interesting, all right."

"Do you think it was symbolic?"

He was still grinning. "No. It was definitely hormones, pure and simple."

Amanda finally relaxed a little and managed to smile. "You're probably right."

Since there were a lot of cars parked in front of Amanda's building, a sleek silver Mercedes among them, Jordan parked almost a block away. It seemed natural to hold hands as they walked back to the entrance.

Amanda was stunned to see James sitting on the bottom step of the stairway leading up to the second floor. He was wearing his usual three-piece tailor-made suit, a necessity for a corporate chief executive officer like himself, and his silver gray hair looked as dashing as ever. His tanned face showed signs of strain, however, and the once-over he gave Jordan was one of cordial contempt.

Amanda's first instinct was to let go of Jordan's hand, but he tightened his grip when she tried.

Meanwhile James had risen from his seat on the stairs. "We have to talk," he said to Amanda.

She shook her head, grateful now for Jordan's presence and his grasp on her hand. "There's nothing to say."

The man she had once loved arched an eyebrow. "Isn't there? You could start by introducing me to the new man in your life."

It was Jordan who spoke. "Jordan Richards," he said evenly, without offering his hand.

James studied him with new interest flickering in his shrewd eyes. "Brockman," he answered. "James Brockman."

A glance at Jordan revealed that he recognized the name—anyone active in the business world would have—but he clearly wasn't the least bit intimidated. He simply nodded an acknowledgment.

Amanda ran her tongue over her lips. "Let us pass, James," she said. She'd never spoken so authoritatively to him before, but she took no pleasure in the achievement because she knew she wouldn't have managed it if Jordan hadn't been there.

James did not look at Amanda, but at Jordan. Some challenge passed between them, and the air was charged with static electricity for several moments. Then James stepped aside to lean against the banister, leaving barely enough room for Jordan and Amanda to walk by.

"Richards."

Jordan stopped, still holding Amanda's hand, and looked back at James over one shoulder in inquiry.

"I'll call your office Monday morning. I'd be interested to know what we have in common—where investments are concerned, naturally."

Amanda felt her face heat. Again she tried to pull away from Jordan; again he restrained her. "Naturally," Jordan responded coldly, and then he continued up the stairway, bringing Amanda with him.

"I'm sorry," she said the moment they were alone in her apartment. She was leaning against the closed door.

"Why?" Jordan asked, reaching out to unbutton her coat. He helped her out of it, then hung it on the brass tree. Amanda watched him with injury in her eyes as he removed his jacket and put it with her coat.

She had been leaning against the door again, and she thrust herself away. "Because of James, of course."

"It wasn't your fault he came here."

She sighed and stopped in the tiny entryway, her back to Jordan, the fingers of one hand pressed to her right temple. She knew he was right, but she was slightly nauseous all the same. "That remark he made about what the two of you might have in common..."

Jordan reached out and took her shoulders in his hands, turning her gently to face him. "Your past is your own business, Amanda. I'm interested in the woman you are now, not the woman you were six months or six years ago."

Amanda blinked, then bit her upper lip for a moment. "But he meant—"

He touched her lip with an index finger. "I know what he meant," he said with hoarse gentleness. "When and if it happens for us, Amanda, you won't be the first woman I've been with. I'm not going to condemn you because I'm not the first man."

With that, the subject of that aspect of Amanda's relationship with James was closed forever. In fact, it was almost as though the subject hadn't been broached. "Would you like some coffee or something?" she asked, feeling better.

Jordan grinned. "Sure."

When Amanda came out of the kitchenette minutes later, carrying two mugs of instant coffee, Jordan was studying the blue-and-white patchwork quilt hanging on the wall behind her couch. Gershwin seemed to have become an appendage to his right ankle.

"Did you make this?"

Amanda nodded proudly. "I designed it, too."

Jordan looked impressed. "So there's more to you than the mild-mannered assistant hotel manager who gets her Christmas shopping done early," he teased.

She smiled. "A little, yes." She extended one mug of coffee and he took it, lifting it to his lips. "I had a good time today, Jordan."

When Amanda sat down on the couch, Jordan did, too. His nearness brought images from the movie they'd seen back to her mind. "So did I," he answered, putting his coffee down on the rickety cocktail table.

*Damn that guy with the ice cube,* Amanda fretted to herself as Jordan put his hands on her shoulders again and slowly drew her close. It seemed to her that a small eternity passed before their lips touched, igniting the soft suspense Amanda felt into a flame of awareness.

The tip of his tongue encircled her lips, and when they parted at his silent bidding, he took immediate advantage. Somehow Amanda found herself lying down on the sofa instead of sitting up, and when Jordan finally pulled away from her mouth, she arched her neck. He kissed the pulse point at the base of her throat, then progressed to the one beneath her right ear. In the meantime, Amanda could feel her T-shirt being worked slowly up her rib cage.

When he unsnapped her bra and laid it aside, revealing her ripe breasts, Amanda closed her eyes and lifted her back slightly in a silent offering.

He encircled one taut nipple with feather-light kisses, and Amanda moaned softly when he captured the morsel between his lips and began to suckle. She entangled her hands in his hair and spread her legs, one foot high on the sofa back, the other on the floor, to accommodate him.

The eloquent pressure of his desire made Amanda ache to be taken, but she was too breathless to speak, too swept up in the gentle incursion to ask for conquering. When she felt the snap on her jeans give way, followed soon after by the zipper, she only lifted her hips so the jeans could be peeled away. They vanished, along with her panties and her sneakers, and Jordan began to caress her intimately with one hand while he enjoyed her other breast.

The ordinary light in the living room turned colors and made strange patterns in front of

Amanda's eyes as Jordan kissed his way down over her satiny, quivering belly to her thighs.

She whimpered when he burrowed into her deepest secret, gave a lusty cry when he plundered that secret with his mouth. Her hips shot upward, and Jordan cupped his hands beneath her bottom, holding her in his hands as he would sparkling water from a stream. "Jordan," she gasped, turning her head from side to side in a fever of passion when he showed her absolutely no mercy.

He flung her over the savage brink, leaving her to convulse repeatedly at the top of an invisible geyser. When the last trace of response had been wrung from her, he lowered her gently back to the sofa.

She lay there watching him, the back of one hand resting against her mouth, her body covered in a fine mist of perspiration. Jordan was sitting up, one of her bare legs draped across his lap, his eyes gentle as he laid a hand on Amanda's trembling belly as if to soothe it.

"I want you," she said brazenly when she could speak.

Jordan smiled and traced the outline of her jaw with one finger, then the circumferences of both her nipples. "Not this time, Mandy," he answered, his voice hardly more than a ragged whisper.

Amanda was both surprised and insulted. "What the hell do you mean, 'not this time'? Were you just trying to prove—"

Jordan interrupted her tirade by bending to kiss her lips. "I wasn't trying to prove anything. I just don't want you hating my guts when you wake up tomorrow."

Amanda's body, so long untouched by a man, was primed for a loving it wasn't going to receive. "You're too late," she spat, bolting to an upright position and righting her bra and T-shirt. "I *already* hate your guts!"

Jordan obligingly fetched her jeans and panties from the floor where he'd tossed them earlier. "Probably, but you'll forgive me when the time is right."

She squirmed back into the rest of her clothes, then stood looking down at Jordan, one finger waggling. "No, I won't!" she argued hotly.

He clasped her hips in his hands and brought her forward, then softly nipped the place he'd just pillaged so sweetly. Even through her jeans, Amanda felt a piercing response to the contact; a shock went through her, and she gave a soft cry of mingled protest and surrender.

Jordan drew back and gave her a swat on the bottom. "See? You'll forgive me."

Amanda would have whirled away then, but Jordan caught her by the hand and wrenched her onto his lap. When she would have risen, he restricted her by catching hold of her hands and imprisoning them behind her back.

With his free hand, he pushed her T-shirt up in front again, then boldly cupped a lace-covered breast that throbbed to be bared to him once more. "It's going to be very good when we make love," he said firmly, "but that isn't going to happen yet."

Amanda squirmed, infuriated and confused. "Then why don't you let me go?" she breathed.

He chuckled. "Because I want to make damn sure you don't forget that preview of how it's going to be."

"Of all the arrogance—"

Jordan pulled down one side of her bra, causing the breast to spring triumphantly to freedom. "I've got plenty of that," he breathed against a peak that strained toward him.

Amanda moaned despite herself when he took her into his mouth again.

"Umm," he murmured, blatant in his enjoyment.

Utter and complete surprise possessed Amanda when she realized she was being propelled to another release, with Jordan merely gripping her hands behind her and feasting on her breast. She didn't want him to know, and yet her body was already betraying her with feverish jerks and twists.

She bit down hard on her lower lip and tried to keep herself still, but she couldn't. She was moving at lightning speed toward a collision with a comet.

Jordan lifted his mouth from her breast just long enough to mutter, "So it's like that, is it?" before driving her hard up against her own nature as a woman.

She surrendered in a burst of surprised gasps and sagged against Jordan, resting her head on his shoulder when it was finally over. "H-how did that happen?"

Still caressing her breast, Jordan spoke against her ear. "No idea," he answered, "but it damned near made me change my mind about waiting."

Amanda lay against his chest until she'd recovered the ability to stand and to breathe properly, then she rose from his lap, snapped her bra and pulled down her T-shirt. In a vain effort to regain her dignity, she squared her shoulders and plunged the splayed fingers of both hands through her hair. "You don't find me attractive—that's it, isn't it?"

"That's the most ridiculous question I've ever been asked," Jordan answered, rising a little awkwardly—and painfully, it seemed to Amanda—from the sofa. "I wouldn't have done the things I just did if I didn't."

"Then why don't you want me?"

"Believe me, I do want you. Too badly to risk lousing things up so soon."

Amanda wasn't satisfied with that answer, so she turned on one heel and fled into the bathroom, where she splashed cold water on her face and brushed her love-tousled hair. When she came out, half fearing that Jordan would be gone, she found him standing at the window, gazing out at the city.

Calmer, she stood behind him, slipped her arms around his lean waist and kissed his nape. "Stay for supper?"

He turned in her embrace to smile down into her eyes. "That depends on what's on the menu."

Amanda was mildly affronted, remembering his rejection. "It isn't me," she stated with a small pout, "so you can relax."

He laughed and gave her another playful swat on the bottom. "Take it from me, Mandy—I'm not relaxed."

She grinned, glad to know he was suffering justly, and kissed his chin, which was already darkening with the shadow of a beard. "Nobody has called me 'Mandy' since first grade," she said.

"Good."

"Why is that good?" Amanda inquired, snuggling close.

"Because it saves me the trouble of thinking up some cutesy nickname like 'babycakes' or 'buttercup.'"

She laughed. "I can't imagine you calling me 'buttercup' with a straight face."

"I don't think I could," he replied, bending his head to kiss her thoroughly. Amanda's knees were weak when he finally drew back.

"You delight in tormenting me," she protested.

His eyes twinkled. "What's for supper?"

"Grilled cheese sandwiches, unless we go to the market," Amanda answered.

"The market it is," Jordan replied. Once again, in the entryway he helped Amanda into her coat.

"You have good manners for a rascal," Amanda remarked quite seriously.

Jordan laughed. "Thank you—I think."

They walked to a small store on the corner, where food was overpriced but fresh and plentiful. Amanda selected two steaks, vegetables for a salad and potatoes for baking.

"Does your fireplace work?" Jordan asked, lingering in front of a display of synthetic logs.

Amanda nodded, wondering if she could stand the romance of a crackling fire when Jordan was so determined not to make love to her. "Are you trying to drive me crazy, or what?" she countered, her eyes snapping with irritation.

He gave her one of his nuclear grins, then picked up two of the logs and carried them to the checkout counter, where he threw down a twenty-dollar bill. He would have paid for the food, too, except that Amanda wouldn't let him.

She did permit him to carry everything back to the apartment, however, thinking it might drain off some of his excess energy.

When they were back in Amanda's apartment, he moved the screen from in front of the fireplace as Gershwin meowed curiously at his elbow. After opening the damper, he laid one of the logs he'd bought in the grate. Amanda glanced at the label on the other log and saw it was meant to last a full three hours.

She grinned as she got her favorite skillet out of the drawer underneath the stove. Two logs totaled six hours. Maybe Jordan would change his mind about waiting before that much time slipped past.

Dusting his hands together, he came into the kitchenette, and Amanda could see the flicker of the fire reflected on the shiny front of her refrigerator door. Without being asked, he took the vegetables out of the bag and began washing them at the sink.

Amanda went to his side, handing him both the potatoes. "You're pretty handy in a kitchen, fella," she remarked in a teasing, sultry voice.

Jordan's eyes danced when he looked at her, and his expression said he was pretty handy in a few other rooms, too. "Thanks." He scrubbed the potatoes and handed them back to Amanda, who put a little swing in her hips as she walked away because she knew he was watching.

He laughed. "You need a spanking."

Amanda poked the potatoes with a fork and set them in the tiny microwave oven her mother and stepfather had given her the Christmas before. "Very kinky, Mr. Richards."

Jordan chuckled as he went back to chopping vegetables, and Amanda found the wooden salad bowl she'd bought in Hawaii and set it on the counter beside him.

They ate at the glass table in Amanda's living room, the fire dancing on the hearth and casting its image on their wineglasses. Darkness had long since settled over the city, and Amanda wondered why she hadn't noticed when the daylight fled.

"Tell me about your daughters," she said when the meal was nearly over.

Jordan pushed his plate away and took a sip of his wine before replying. "They're normal kids, I guess. They like to watch *Sesame Street*, have me read the funny papers to them, things like that."

Amanda felt sad, but if someone had asked, she would have had to admit she wasn't thinking about Jordan's children at all. She was remembering how it felt when her dad had gone away that long-ago Christmas Day, swearing never to come back. And he hadn't. "Do you miss them?" she asked.

"Yes," he admitted frankly. "But I know they're better off with Karen and Paul."

"Why?" Amanda dared to ask.

Jordan lifted his shoulders in a slight shrug. "I told you—my sister and her husband took them in when I was in the hospital. I'm more like an uncle to them than a father. They wouldn't understand if I uprooted them now."

Amanda wasn't so sure, but she didn't say that because she knew she'd already overstepped her bounds in some ways. If Jordan didn't want to raise his own children, that was his business, but it made Amanda wonder what would happen if the two of them were ever married and had babies. If she died, would he just send the kids to live with someone else?

She refilled her wineglass and took a healthy sip.

There was a look of quiet understanding in Jordan's eyes as he watched her. "What have I done now?" he asked.

"Nothing," Amanda lied, setting her glass down and jumping up to begin clearing the table.

Jordan rose from his chair and elbowed her aside. "Go and sit by the fire. I'll take care of this."

Apparently giving orders had become a habit with Jordan over the course of his successful career. "I'll help," she insisted, following him into the kitchen with the salad bowl in her hands.

Jordan scraped and rinsed the plates, and Amanda put them, along with the silverware and glasses, into the dishwasher.

"Somebody trained you rather well," she commented grudgingly.

He gave her a meltdown grin. "Thanks for noticing," he said with a slight leer.

Amanda's face turned pink. "I was talking about cooking and doing dishes!"

Jordan smiled at her discomfiture. "Oh," he said, but he sounded patently unconvinced.

Amanda put what remained of the salad in a smaller bowl, covered that tightly with plastic wrap, then stuck it into the refrigerator. She longed to ask him what kind of wife Becky had been, but she didn't dare. She knew he'd say she'd been wonderful, and Amanda wasn't feeling grown-up enough to deal with that.

He was leaning against the sink, watching her, his arms folded in front of his chest. "James is a lot older than you are," he said.

The remark was so out of left field that Amanda was momentarily stunned by it. "I know," she finally managed, standing in the doorway that led to the living room.

"Where did you meet him?"

Amanda couldn't think why she was answering, since they had agreed not to talk about James, but answer she did. "At the hotel," she replied with a sigh. "He taught a management seminar there a year and a half ago."

"And you went?"

She couldn't read Jordan's mood either in his eyes or his voice, and she was unsettled by the question. "Yes. He asked me out to dinner the first night, and after that I saw him whenever he was in Seattle on business."

Jordan crossed the room and enfolded Amanda in his arms, and the relief she felt was totally out of proportion to the circumstances.

"I have to know one thing, Mandy. Do you love him?"

She shook her head. "No." She tasted wine on Jordan's lips when he kissed her. And she tasted wanting. *Do you still love Becky?* she longed to ask, but she was too afraid of the answer to voice the question.

Slipping his arm around her waist, Jordan ushered Amanda into the living room, where they sat on a hooked rug in front of the fireplace. He gripped her hand and stared into the flames in the silence for a long time, then he turned, looked into her fire-lit eyes and said, "I'm sorry, Mandy. I didn't have any right to ask about James."

She let her head rest against the place where his arm and shoulder met. "It's okay. I made a fool of myself, and I can admit that now."

Jordan caught her chin in his hand and wouldn't let her look away. "Let's get one thing straight here," he said in gentle reproach. "The only mistake you made was trusting the bastard. He's the fool."

Amanda sighed. "That's a refreshing opinion. Most people either say or imply that I should have known better."

"Not this people," Jordan answered, tasting her lips.

Although it seemed impossible, Amanda wanted Jordan more now than she had on the couch earlier when he'd brought her face to face with her own womanhood. She longed to take him by the hand and lead him to her bed, but the thought of a second rebuff stopped her. In fact, she supposed it was about time she started taking the advice her mother had given her in ninth grade and play hard to get.

She moved a little apart from Jordan, stiffened her shoulders and raised her chin. "Maybe you should go," she said.

Jordan showed no signs of leaving. Instead he put his hands on Amanda's shoulders and lowered her to the hooked rug, stretching out beside her and laying one hand brazenly on her breast. The nipple tightened obediently beneath his palm.

Amanda moved to rise, but Jordan pressed her back down again, this time with a consuming kiss. "Don't you dare start anything you don't intend to finish," she ordered in a raspy whisper when at last he'd drawn away from her mouth. Having obtained the response he wanted from her right breast, he was now working on her left.

"I'll finish it," he vowed in a husky murmur, "when the time is right."

He lowered his hand to her belly, covering it with splayed fingers, and Amanda's heart pounded beneath her T-shirt. She pulled on his nape until his mouth again joined with hers, and the punishment for this audacious act was the unsnapping of her jeans.

"Damn it, Jordan, I don't like being teased."

He pulled at the zipper, and then his hand was in between her jeans and her panties, just resting there, soaking up her warmth, making her grow moist. That part of her body was like an exotic orchid flowering in a hothouse.

"Tough," he replied with a cocky grin just before he bent and scraped one hidden nipple lightly with his teeth, causing it to leap to attention.

Amanda's formidable pride was almost gone, and she had to grasp the rug and bite down on her lower lip to keep from begging him to make love to her.

"This night is just for you," he told her, his hand making a fiery circle at the junction of her thighs. "Why can't you accept that?"

"Because it isn't normal, that's why," Amanda gasped, trying to hold her hips still but finding it impossible. "You're a man. You're supposed to have just one thing on your mind. You're supposed to be trying to jump my bones."

He laughed at that. "What a chauvinistic thing to say."

Amanda groaned as he continued his sweet devilment. "I've never seen anything in *Cosmopolitan* that told what to d-do when this happens," she complained.

Again Jordan laughed. "I can tell you what to do," he said when he'd recovered himself a little. "Enjoy it."

Amanda was beginning to breathe hard. "Damn you, Jordan—I'll make you pay for this!"

"I'm counting on that," he said against her mouth.

Moments later Amanda was soaring again. She dug her fingers into Jordan's shoulders while she plunged her heels into the rug, and everyone in the apartment building would have known how well he'd loved her if he hadn't clamped his mouth over hers and swallowed her cries.

\* \* \*

"If this is some kind of power game," Amanda sputtered five minutes later when she could manage to speak, fastening her jeans and sitting up again, "I don't want to play."

"You could have fooled me," Jordan responded.

Amanda gave a strangled cry of frustration and anger. "I can't imagine why I keep letting you get away with this."

"I can," he replied. "It feels good, and it's been a long time. Right?"

Amanda let her forehead rest against his shoulder, embarrassed. "Yes," she confessed.

He kissed the top of her head. "I should have dessert before dinner more often," he teased.

Amanda groaned, unable to look at him, and he chuckled and lifted her chin for a light kiss. "You're impossible," she murmured.

"And I'm leaving," he added with a glance at his watch. "It's time you were in bed."

Bleakness filled Amanda at the thought of climbing into bed alone, and she was just about to protest, when Jordan laid a finger to her nose and asked, "Will you go Christmas shopping with me tomorrow?"

Amanda would have gone to Zanzibar. "Yes," she answered like a hypnotized person.

Jordan kissed her again, leaving her lips warm and slightly swollen. "Good night," he said. And then, after a backward look and a wave, he was gone.

# 4

The telephone jangled just as Amanda finished with her makeup the next morning. She'd managed to camouflage the shadows under her eyes—the result of sleeping only a few hours—with a cover stick.

"Hello?" she blurted into the receiver of her bedside telephone, hoping Jordan wasn't calling to back out of their shopping trip.

"If I remember correctly," her mother began dryly without returning the customary greeting, "you were supposed to call last night and let us know whether you were coming over for supper."

Amanda stretched the phone cord as far as her closet, where she took out black wool slacks. "Sorry, Mom," she answered contritely. "I forgot, but you'll be glad to know it was because of a man." She went to the dresser for her pink cashmere sweater while waiting for her mother to digest her last remark.

"A man?" Marion echoed, unable to hide the pleasure in her voice.

"And James was here yesterday," Amanda went on after pulling the sweater on over her head.

Marion drew in her breath. "Don't tell me you're seeing him again—"

"Of course not, Mom," Amanda scolded, propping the receiver between her shoulder and her ear while she wriggled into the sleek black pants.

"You're deliberately confusing me," Marion accused.

Amanda sighed. "Listen, I'll tell you everything tomorrow, okay? I'll stop by after work and catch you up on all the latest developments."

"So there is somebody besides James?" Marion pressed, sounding pleased.

"Yep," Amanda answered just as the door buzzer sounded. "Gotta go—he's here."

"'Bye," Marion said cooperatively, and promptly hung up.

Amanda was brushing her hair as she hurried through the apartment to open the door. She was smiling, since she expected Jordan, but she found a delivery man from one of the more posh department stores in the hallway, instead. He was holding two silver gift boxes, one large and one fairly small. "Ms. A. Scott?" he asked.

Amanda nodded, mystified.

"These are for you—special express delivery," the man said, holding on to the packages while he shoved a clipboard at Amanda. "Sign on line twenty-seven."

She found the appropriate line and scrawled her name there, and the man gave her the packages in return for the clipboard.

After depositing the boxes on the couch and rummaging through her purse for a tip, she closed the door and lifted the lid off the smaller box. A skimpy aqua bikini lay inside, but there was no card or note to explain.

She opened the large box and gasped, faced with the rich, unmistakable splendor of sable. A small envelope lay on top, but Amanda didn't need to read it to know the gifts were from James.

As a matter of curiosity, she looked at the card: "Honeymoon in Hawaii, then on to Copenhagen? Call me. James."

With a sigh, Amanda tossed down the card. She was just about to call the store and ask to return the two boxes, when there was a knock at the door.

She rushed to open it and found Jordan standing in the hallway, looking spectacular in blue jeans, a lightweight yellow sweater and a tweed sport jacket.

"Hi," he said, his bright hazel eyes registering approval as he looked at her.

"Come in," Amanda replied, stepping back and holding the door open wide. "I'm just about finished with my hair. Pour yourself a cup of coffee and I'll be right out."

He stopped her when she would have turned away from him, and lightly entangled the fingers of one hand in her hair. "Don't change it," he said hoarsely. "It looks great."

Amanda's heart was beating a little faster just because he was close and because he was touching her. Since she didn't know what to say, she didn't speak.

Jordan kissed her lightly on the lips. "Good morning, Mandy," he said, and his voice was still husky. Amanda had a vision of him carrying her off to bed, and heat flooded her entire body, a blush rising in her cheeks.

"Good morning," she replied, her voice barely more than a squeak. "How about that coffee?"

His gaze had shifted to the boxes on the couch. "What's this?" There was a teasing reproach in his eyes when they returned to her face. "Opening your presents before Christmas, Mandy? For shame."

Amanda had completely forgotten the unwanted gifts, and the reminder deflated her spirits a little. "I'm sending them back," she said, hoping Jordan wouldn't pursue the subject.

His expression sobered. "James?"

Amanda licked her lips, then nodded nervously. She wasn't entirely displeased to see a muscle in Jordan's cheek grow taut, then relax again.

"Persistent, isn't he?"

"Yes," Amanda admitted. "He is." And after that there seemed to be nothing more to say—about James, anyway.

"Let's go," Jordan told her, kissing her forehead. "We'll get some breakfast on the way."

Amanda disappeared into the bedroom to put on her shoes, and when she came out, Jordan was studying the quilt over her couch again, his hands in his hip pockets.

"You know, you have a real talent for this," he said.

Amanda smiled. James had always been impatient with her quilting, saying she ought to save the needlework for when she was old and had nothing better to do. "Thanks."

Jordan followed her out of the apartment and waited patiently while she locked the door. He held her elbow lightly as they went down the stairs, once again giving her the wonderful sensation of being protected.

The sun was shining, which was cause for rejoicing in Seattle at that time of year, and Amanda felt happy as Jordan closed the car door after her.

When he slid behind the wheel, he just sat there for a few minutes and looked at her. Then he put a hand in her hair again. "Excuse me, lady," he said, his voice low, "but has anybody told you this morning that you're beautiful?"

Amanda flushed, but her eyes were sparkling. "No, sir," she answered, playing the game. "They haven't."

He leaned toward her and gave her a lingering kiss that made a sweet languor blossom inside her.

"There's an oversight that needs correcting," he murmured afterward. "You're beautiful."

Amanda was trembling when he finally turned to start the ignition, fasten his seat belt and steer the car out into the light Sunday morning traffic. Something was terribly wrong in this relationship, she reflected. It was supposed to be the man who wanted to head straight for the bedroom, while the woman held out for knowing each other better.

And yet it was all Amanda could do not to drag Jordan out of the car and back up the stairs to her apartment.

"What's the matter?" Jordan asked, tossing a mischievous glance her way that said he well knew the answer to that question.

Amanda folded her arms and looked straight ahead as they sped up a freeway ramp. The familiar green-and-white signs slipped by overhead. "Nothing," she said.

He sighed. "I hate it when women do that. You ask them what's wrong and they say 'nothing,' and all the while you know they're ready to burst into tears or clout you with the nearest blunt object."

Amanda turned in her seat and studied his profile for a few moments, one fingernail caught between her teeth. "I wasn't about to do either of those things," she finally said. She didn't quite have the fortitude to go the rest of the way and admit she was wondering why he didn't seem to want her.

Jordan reached out and laid a hand gently on her knee, once again sending all her vital organs into a state of alarm.

"What's the problem, then?"

She drew in a deep breath for courage and let it out slowly. "If we sleep together, you'll be the second man I've ever been with in my life, so it's not like I'm hot to trot or anything. But I usually have to fight guys off, not wait for them to decide the time is right."

He was clearly suppressing a smile, which didn't help.

"'Hot to trot'? I didn't think anybody said that anymore."

"Jordan."

He favored her with a high-potency grin. "Believe me, Mandy, I'm a normal man and I want you. But you're going to have to wait, because I've got no intention of—forgive me—screwing this up."

Amanda sighed and folded her arms. "Exactly what is it you're waiting for?"

His wonderful eyes were crinkled with laughter, even though his mouth was unsmiling.

"Exactly what is it you want me to do?" he countered. "Pull the car over to the side of the freeway and, as you put it last night, 'jump your bones'?"

Amanda blushed. "You make me sound like some kind of loose woman," she accused.

He took her hand and squeezed it reassuringly. "I can't even imagine that," he said in a soothing voice. "Now what do you say we change the subject for a while?"

That seemed like the only solution. "Okay," Amanda agreed. "Remember how you admired the quilt I made?"

Jordan nodded, switching lanes to be in position for an upcoming exit. "It's great."

"Well, I've been designing and making quilts for years. Someday I hope to open a bed and breakfast somewhere, with a little craft shop on the premises."

He grinned as he took the exit. "I'm surprised. Given your job and the fact that you live in the city, I thought you were inclined toward more sophisticated dreams.''

"I was," Amanda said, recalling some of the glamorous, exciting adventures she had had with James. "But life changes a person. And I've always liked making quilts. I've been selling them at craft shows for a long time, and saving as much money as I could for the bed and breakfast."

Jordan was undoubtedly thinking of her humble apartment when he said, ''You must have a pretty solid nest egg.''

Amanda sighed, feeling discouraged all over again. ''Not really. The real estate market is hot around here, what with so many people moving up from California, and the prices are high.''

They had left the freeway, and Jordan pulled the car into the parking lot of a family-style restaurant near the mall. "Working capital is one of my specialties, Mandy. Maybe I can help you."

Amanda surprised even herself when she shook her head so fast. She guessed it was partly pride that made her do that, and partly disappointment that he wasn't trying to talk her out of establishing a business in favor of something else. Like getting married and starting a family.

"Did we just hit another tricky subject?" Jordan asked good-naturedly, when he and Amanda were walking toward the restaurant.

She shrugged. "I want the bed and breakfast to be all my own."

Jordan opened the door for her. "What if you decide to get married or something?"

Amanda felt a little thrill, even though she knew Jordan wasn't on the verge of proposing. She would have refused even if he had. "I guess I'll cross that bridge when I come to it."

A few minutes later they were seated at a small table and given menus. They made their selections and sipped the coffee the waitress had brought while they waited for the food.

"Who are we shopping for today?" Amanda asked, to get the conversation going again. Jordan was sitting across from her, systematically making love to her with his eyes, and she was desperate to distract him.

"Jessie and Lisa mostly, though I still need to get something for Karen and Paul."

Something made Amanda ask, "What about your parents?"

Sadness flickered in the depths of Jordan's eyes, but only for a moment. "They were killed in a car accident when I was in college," he replied.

Amanda reached out on impulse and took his hand. It seemed to her that Jordan had had more than his share of tragedy in his life, and she suddenly wanted to share her mother and stepfather with him. "I'm sorry."

He changed the subject so abruptly his remark was almost a rebuff. "What do you think Karen would like?"

Amanda was annoyed and a little hurt. "How would I know? I've never even met the woman."

The waitress returned with their breakfast, setting bacon and eggs in front of Jordan and giving Amanda wheat toast and a fruit compote. When they were alone again, Jordan replied, "Karen's thirty-five, a little on the chubby side—and totally devoted to Paul and the girls."

Amanda tried to picture the woman and failed. "Do she and Paul have children of their own?"

Jordan was mashing his eggs into his hash browns. "No."

She speared a melon ball and chewed it distractedly. "That's sad," she said after swallowing.

"These things happen," Jordan replied.

Amanda looked straight into his eyes. "I guess Karen would be pretty upset if she ever had to give Jessica and Lisa back to you," she ventured to say.

He returned her bold, assessing stare. "I wouldn't do that to her or to the girls," he said, and there was no hint of mischief about him this time. He was completely serious.

Things were a little strained between them throughout the rest of the meal, but as soon as they reached the toy store at the mall, they were both caught up in the spirit of the season. They bought games for the girls, and dolls, and little china tea sets.

Amanda couldn't remember the last time she'd had so much fun, and her eyes were sparkling as they stuffed everything into the back of the Porsche.

From the toy store they headed to a big-name department store where, after great deliberation, they chose expensive perfume and bath powder for Karen and a sweater for her husband.

They had lunch in a fast-food hamburger place jammed to the rafters with excited kids, and by the time they returned to Amanda's apartment, she was exhausted.

"Coming in?" she asked at the door because, in spite of everything he'd said about waiting, she'd been entertaining a discreet fantasy all morning.

Jordan shook his head. "Not today," he said. "I've got to drive up to Port Townsend and look in on the kids."

Amanda was hurt that he didn't want to take her along, but she hid it well. After all, she didn't have the right to any injured feelings. "Say hello for me," she said softly.

He kissed her, lightly at first, then with an authority that brought the fantasy to the forefront of her mind. Amanda surreptitiously gripped the doorknob to keep from sliding to the floor.

"I'll be out of town most of next week," he said when the kiss was over. "Is it okay if I call?"

*Is it okay?* She would be shattered if he didn't. "Sure," she answered in a tone that said it wouldn't matter one way or the other because she'd be busy with her glamorous, sophisticated life.

Jordan waited until she'd unlocked the door and stepped safely inside, then she heard him walking away.

She tossed aside her purse, kicked off her shoes and hung up her coat. The coming week yawned before her like an abyss.

Ignoring the boxes still sitting on her couch, she bent distractedly to pet a meowing Gershwin, then stumbled into her bedroom, stripped off her clothes and crawled back into the unmade bed. All those hours she hadn't slept the night before were catching up with her.

Later she awoke to full darkness, the weight of Gershwin curled up on her stomach and the ringing of the phone.

Groping with one hand, she found the receiver, brought it to her ear and yawned, "Hello?"

"It's Mom," Marion announced. "How are you, dear?"

Amanda yawned again. "Tired. And hungry."

"Perfect," Marion responded with her customary good cheer and indefatigable energy.

"Drag yourself over here, and I'll serve you a home-cooked meal that will put hair on your chest."

Amanda giggled, rubbing her eyes and stretching. The movement made Gershwin jump down from her stomach and land with a solid *thump* on the floor. "There's one flaw in your proposal, Mom. Who needs hair on their chest?"

Marion laughed. "Just get in your car and drive over here. Or should I send Bob, so you don't have to go wandering around in that dark parking lot behind your building?"

"There's an attendant," Amanda said, sitting up. "I'll drive over as soon as I've had a quick shower to revive myself."

Marion agreed, and the conversation came to an amicable end.

With her hair pulled back into a ponytail, Amanda was wearing jeans, a football jersey and sneakers when she arrived at her parents' house in another part of the city. And she was making a determined effort not to think about Jordan and the fact that he hadn't asked her to go to Port Townsend with him.

Her mother, a slender, attractive woman with shoulder-length hennaed hair and skillfully applied makeup, met her at the front door. Marion looked wonderful in her trim green jumpsuit, and her smile and hug were both warm.

"Bob's in the living room, cussing that string of Christmas tree lights that always goes on the blink," the older woman confided in a merry whisper.

Amanda laughed and wandered into the front room. There were cards everywhere—they lined the top of the piano, the mantel and were arranged into the shape of a Christmas tree on one wall. Amanda had been putting hers in a desk drawer that year.

"Hi, Bob," she said, giving her stepfather a hug. He was a tall man, with thinning blond hair and kindly blue eyes, and he'd been very good to Marion. Amanda loved him for that reason, if for no other.

He was standing beside a fresh-smelling, undecorated pine tree, which was, as usual, set up in front of the bay window facing the street. The infamous string of lights was in his hands. "I don't know why she won't let me throw these darned things out and buy new ones," he fussed in a conspiratorial whisper. "It's not as if we couldn't afford to."

Amanda chuckled. "Mom's sentimental about those lights," she reminded him. "They've been on the tree since Eunice and I were babies."

"Speaking of your sister," Marion remarked from the kitchen doorway, wiping her hands on her white apron, ''we had a call from her today. She's coming home for Christmas.''

Amanda was pleased. This was a hard time in Eunice's life; she needed to get away from the wreckage of her marriage, if only for a week or two. ''What about her job at the university?''

Marion shrugged. ''I guess she's taking time off. Bob and I are picking her up at the airport late next Friday night.''

Amanda left Bob to his Christmas tree light quandary and followed her mother into the bright, fragrant kitchen, where they had had so many talks before. ''Seattle will be a shock to Eunice after Southern California,'' she remarked.

Marion gave her a playful flick with a dish towel. ''Forget the harmless chitchat,'' she said with a grin. ''What's going on in your life these days? Who's the new man, and what the devil was James doing, dropping by?''

Drawing up a battered metal stool, Amanda sat down at the breakfast counter Bob had built when he remodeled the kitchen, and started cutting up the salad vegetables her mother indicated. ''James is getting divorced,'' she said, avoiding Marion's gaze. ''Evidently he has some idea that we can get back together.''

''I presume you set him straight on that.''

''I did.'' Amanda sighed. ''But I'm not sure he's getting the message. He sent me a sable jacket and a silk bikini today, along with an invitation to Hawaii and Copenhagen.''

The oven door slammed a touch too hard after Marion pulled a pan of fragrant lasagna from it. ''You'd never guess he was such a scumbag, would you?''

Amanda grinned and tossed a handful of chopped celery into the salad bowl. ''You've got to stop watching all those cop shows, Mom. It's affecting your vocabulary.''

''No way,'' replied Marion, who had a minor crush on Don Johnson. ''So, who's the other guy?''

''Did I say there was another guy?''

''I think so,'' Marion replied airily, ''but you wouldn't have had to. There's a sparkle in your eyes and your cheeks are pink.''

''His name is Jordan Richards,'' Amanda said. Personally she attributed any sparkle in her eyes or color in her cheeks to the nap she'd taken.

Marion stopped slicing the lasagna to look directly at her daughter. ''And?''

''And he makes me crazy, that's what.''

Marion beamed. ''That's a good sign.''

Amanda wondered if her mother would still be of the same opinion if she knew just how hard her daughter had fallen. And how bold she'd been. ''I guess so.''

"What does he do for a living?" Bob asked from the kitchen doorway. Since it was a classic parental question, Amanda didn't take offense.

"He's a partner in an investment firm—Striner, Striner and Richards."

Bob whistled and tucked his hands in his pockets. "That's the big time, all right."

"Amanda doesn't care how much money he makes," Marion said with mock haughtiness. "She just wants his body."

At this, both Amanda and Bob laughed.

"Mom!" Amanda protested.

"It's true," Marion insisted. "I'd know that look anywhere. Now let's all sit down and eat."

They trooped into the dining room, where Marion had set a festive table using the special Christmas dishes that always came out of storage, along with the nativity set, on the first of December. Despite the good food and the conversation, Amanda's mind was on Jordan.

"About those presents James sent you," Marion began when she and Amanda were alone in the kitchen again, washing dishes while Bob fought it out with the Christmas tree lights. "You are sending them back, aren't you?"

Amanda favored her mother with a rueful smile. "Of course I am. First thing tomorrow."

"Some women would have their heads turned, you know, by such expensive things."

"Expensive is right. All James wants in return for his presents is my soul. What a bargain."

Marion finished washing the last pot, drained the sink and washed her hands. "I'm glad you're wise enough to see that."

Amanda shrugged. "I don't know how smart I am," she replied. "The only reason I'm so sure about everything where James is concerned is that I don't love him anymore. I'm not sure what I'd do if I still cared."

"I am," Marion said confidently. "You've always had a good head on your shoulders. That's why I think this new man must really be something."

Amanda indulged in a smile as she shook out the dish towel and hung it on the rack to dry. "He is." But her smile faded as she thought of those two little girls living far away from their father with an aunt and uncle, and of Becky, cut down before she'd even had a chance to live.

"What is it?" Marion wanted to know. She had already poured two cups full of coffee, and she carried them to the kitchen table while waiting for Amanda to answer.

Amanda sank dejectedly into one of the chairs and cupped her hands around a steaming mug. "He's a widower, and I think—well, I think he might have some problems with commitment."

"Don't they all?" Marion asked, stirring artificial sweetener into her coffee.

"Bob didn't," Amanda pointed out, her voice solemn. "He loved you enough to marry you, even though he knew you had two teenage daughters and a pile of debts."

Marion looked thoughtful. "How long have you known this man?"

"Not very long," Amanda confessed. "About ten days, I guess."

Marion chuckled and shook her head. "And you're already bandying words like 'commitment' about?"

"No. I'm only *thinking* words like 'commitment.'"

"I see. Well, this is serious. Why do you think he wouldn't want to settle down?"

Amanda ran the tip of her index finger around the rim of her coffee mug. "He has two little girls, and they don't live with him—his sister and brother-in-law are raising them. He sort of bristled when I asked him about it."

Marion laid a hand on her daughter's arm. "You're a little gun-shy, dear, and that's natural after what happened with James. Just give yourself some time."

*Time.* Jordan was asking the same thing of her. Didn't anyone act on impulse anymore?

Marion smiled at her daughter's frustrated expression. "Just take life one day at a time, Amanda, and everything will work out."

Amanda nodded, and after chatting briefly with her mother about Eunice's upcoming visit, she put on her coat, kissed both her parents goodbye and went out to her nondescript car.

"You be careful to park where the attendant can see you," Bob instructed her just before she pulled away from the curb.

The attendant was on duty, and Amanda parked where there was plenty of light.

It turned out, however, that it was the inside of her building that she should have looked out for, not the parking lot.

James was sitting on the stairs again, and this time she didn't have Jordan along to act as a buffer.

"I'm glad you're here," Amanda said in a cold voice. "You can take back the fur and the bikini."

James's handsome, distinguished face fell. "You still haven't forgiven me, have you?" he asked in a pained voice, spreading his hands wide for emphasis. "Baby, how many times do I have to tell you? Madge and I haven't been in love for years."

Amanda ached as she remembered Madge Brockman's raging agony during the confrontation. "Maybe *you* haven't been," she muttered sadly.

James either didn't hear the remark or chose to ignore it. "Just let me talk to you. Please."

Having summoned up the courage she needed, Amanda passed him on the narrow stairway. "Nothing you can say will change my mind, James." She reached her door and unlocked it as he made to follow her. "So just take your presents and give them to some other fool."

Suddenly James caught her elbow in a hard grasp and wrenched her around to face him. "You're in love with Richards, aren't you? The boy wonder! You think he's pretty hot stuff, I'll bet! Well, let me tell you something—I could buy and sell him ten times over!"

Amanda pulled free of James, stormed over to the couch, picked up the boxes and shoved them at him. "Take these and get out!"

He stared at her as though she'd lost her mind.

"And while you're at it, you can just take everything *else* you've ever given me, too!"

With that, she strode into the bedroom and yanked open her jewelry box, intending to return the gold bracelet and pearl earrings she'd forgotten about. She only became aware that James had followed her when he cried out.

Turning, Amanda saw him clasp his chest with one hand and topple to the floor.

# 5

James's face was contorted with pain, and he was only partially conscious. "Help—me—" he groaned.

Amanda lunged for the phone on her bedside table, punched 911 and barked out her address when someone came on the line. She followed that with a brief description of the problem.

"Someone will be there in a few minutes," the woman on the telephone assured her. "Is the patient conscious?"

James was clearly in agony, but he was awake. "Yes."

"Then just cover him up and make him as comfortable as you can—and try to reassure him. The paramedics will take care of everything else when they get there."

Amanda hung up and draped James with a quilt dragged from her bed. When it was in place, she knelt beside him and grasped his hand.

"It's going to be okay, James," she said, her eyes stinging with tears. "Everything is going to be okay."

His free hand was clenched against his chest. "Hurts—so much . . . crushing . . ."

"I know," Amanda whispered, holding his knuckles to her lips. She could hear sirens in the distance. "Help will be here soon."

A loud knock sounded at the door just a few minutes later.

"In here!" Amanda called, and soon two paramedics burst into the bedroom, bringing a stretcher and some other equipment. She scrambled out of the way and perched on the end of her bed, still unmade from her nap earlier, watching as James was examined, loaded onto the stretcher and given oxygen and an IV.

"Any history of heart disease?" one of the men asked Amanda as he and his partner lifted the stretcher.

"I—I don't know," Amanda whispered.

"We'll be taking him to Harborview Hospital, if you'd like to come along," the other volunteered.

Amanda only sat there, gripping the edge of the mattress and shaking her head, unable to tell them she wasn't James's wife.

When the telephone rang a full hour later, she was still sitting in the exact same place.

"H-hello?"

Jordan's voice was warm and low. "Hello, Mandy. Is something wrong?"

Amanda dragged her forearm across her face, wiping away tears that had long since dried. *James had a heart attack in my bedroom,* she imagined herself answering.

She couldn't explain the situation to Jordan over the phone, she decided, sinking her teeth into her lower lip.

"Mandy?" Jordan prompted when the silence had stretched on too long.

"I thought you were in Port Townsend," she managed in a small voice that was hoarse from crying.

"I just got back," he answered. "As a matter of fact, I'm spending the night in a hotel out by the airport, since my plane leaves so early tomorrow."

Amanda swallowed hard and did her best to sound ordinary. There would be time enough to tell Jordan what had happened when he got back from his business trip. "Wh-where are you going?"

"Chicago. Mandy, what's the matter?"

She closed her eyes. "We can talk about it when you get home."

There was a long pause while he digested that. "Is this something I should know about?"

Amanda nodded, even though he wasn't there to see her. "Yes," she admitted, "but I can't talk about it like this. I have to be with you."

"I could get in the car and be there in half an hour."

Amanda would have given anything short of her very soul to have Jordan there in the room with her, to be held and comforted by him. But she'd only known him a little while, and she had no right to make demands. "I'll be okay," she said softly.

After that, there didn't seem to be much to say. Jordan promised to phone her from Chicago the first chance he got and Amanda wished him well, then the call was over.

Amanda had barely replaced the receiver, when the bell jangled again, startling her. If it had been Jordan she would have relented and asked him to come over, but the voice on the other end of the line was a woman's.

"Well, I must say, I half expected you to be at the hospital, clutching James's hand and swearing your undying love."

Amanda closed her eyes again, feeling as though she'd been struck. The caller was Madge Brockman, James's estranged wife. "Mrs. Brockman, I—"

"Don't lie to me, please. I just spoke to someone on the hospital staff, and they told me James had suffered a heart attack 'at the home of a friend.' It didn't take a genius to figure out just who that 'friend' might be.''

Deciding to let the innuendos pass unchallenged, Amanda asked, ''Is James going to be all right?''

''He's in critical condition. I'm flying in tonight to sit with him.''

It was a relief to know James wouldn't be going through this difficult time alone. ''Mrs. Brockman, I'm very sorry—for everything.''

The woman hung up with a slam, leaving Amanda holding the receiver in one trembling hand and listening to a dial tone. Slowly she put down the phone, then crouched to unplug it from the outlet. After disconnecting the living room phone, as well, she took a long, hot shower and crawled into bed.

The sound of her alarm and faceful of bright sunshine woke her early the next morning. The memory of James lying on her bedroom floor in terrible pain was still all too fresh in her mind.

But Amanda had a job, so, even though she would have preferred to stay in bed with her face turned to the wall, she fed the cat, showered, dressed and put on makeup. Once she'd pinned her hair up in a businesslike chignon, she reconnected the telephones and called the hospital.

James was in stable condition.

Longing for Jordan, who might have been able to put the situation into some kind of perspective, Amanda pulled on her coat and gloves and left her apartment.

Late that afternoon, just as she was preparing to go home for the day, Jordan called. He was getting ready to have dinner with some clients, and there was something clipped about his voice. Something distant.

"Feeling better?" he asked.

Amanda heard a whole glacier of emotion shifting beneath the tip of the iceberg. "Not a whole lot," she admitted, "but it's nothing for you to worry about."

She could almost see him hooking his cuff links. "I read about James in the afternoon edition of the paper, Amanda."

So he knew about the heart attack, and she was no longer 'Mandy.' "Word gets around," she managed, propping one elbow on her desk and sinking her forehead into her palm.

"Is that what you didn't want to talk about last night?"

There was no point in trying to evade the question further. "Yes. It happened in my bedroom, Jordan."

He was quiet for a long time. Much too long.

"Jordan?"

"I'm here. What was he doing in your bedroom, or don't I have the right to ask?"

Tears were brimming in Amanda's eyes, and she prayed no one would step into her office and catch her displaying such unprofessional emotions. "Of course you have the right. He came over because he wanted to persuade me to start seeing him again. I told him to take back the things he gave me, and then I remembered some jewelry he'd given me a long time ago. I went to get them, and he followed me." She drew in a shaky breath, then let it out again. "He got very angry, and he was yelling at me. He just—just fell to the floor."

"My God," Jordan rasped. "What kind of shape is he in now?"

"When I called the hospital this morning, he was stable."

Jordan's voice was husky. "Mandy, I'm sorry."

Amanda didn't know whether he meant he was sorry for doubting her, or he was sorry about James's misfortune. "I wish you were here," she said, testing the water. Everything would ride on his reply.

"So do I," he answered.

Relief flooded over Amanda. "You're not angry?"

He sighed. "No. I guess I just lost my head for a little while there. Do you want me to come back tonight, Mandy? There's a flight at midnight."

"No." She shook her head. "Stay there and set the financial world on its ear. I'll be okay."

"Promise?"

For the first time since before James's collapse, Amanda smiled. "I promise."

"In that case, I'll be back sometime on Friday night. How about penciling me into your busy schedule, Ms. Scott?"

Amanda chuckled. "Consider yourself penciled."

"In fact," he went on, "have a bag packed. I'll stop and pick you up on my way home from the airport."

"Have a bag packed?" Amanda echoed. "Wait a minute, Jordan. What are you proposing here?"

He hesitated only a moment before answering, "I want you to spend the weekend at my place."

Amanda's throat tightened. "Is this the Jordan I know—the one who insists on taking things slow and easy?"

"The same," Jordan replied, his words husky. "I need to have you under the same roof with me, Mandy. Whether we sleep together is entirely up to you."

She plucked some tissue from the box on her desk and began wiping away the mascara stains on her cheeks. "That's mighty mannerly of you, Mr. Richards," she drawled.

"See you Friday," he replied.

And after just a few more words, Amanda hung up.

It was some time before she got out of her chair, though. She'd had some violent ups and downs in the past twenty-four hours, and her emotional equilibrium was not what it might have been.

After taking a few minutes to sit with her head resting on her folded arms, Amanda finished up a report she'd been working on, then slipped into the ladies' room to repair her makeup. Leaving the elevator on the first floor of the hotel, she encountered Madge Brockman.

Mrs. Brockman was a slender, attractive brunette, expensively dressed and clearly well educated. There were huge shadows under her eyes.

"Hello, Amanda," she said.

At first Amanda thought it was just extraordinarily bad luck that she'd run into Mrs. Brockman, but moments later she realized the woman had been waiting in the lobby for her. "Hello, Mrs. Brockman. How is James?"

James's wife reached for Amanda's arm, then let her hand fall back to her side. "I was wondering if you wouldn't have a drink with me or something," she said awkwardly. "So we could talk."

Amanda took a deep breath. "If there's going to be a scene—"

Madge shook her head quickly. "There won't be, I promise."

Hoping Mrs. Brockman meant what she'd said, Amanda followed her into the cocktail lounge, where they took a quiet table in a corner. When the waiter came, Amanda asked for a diet cola and Mrs. Brockman ordered a gin and tonic.

"The doctor tells me James is going to live," Mrs. Brockman said when the drinks had arrived and the waiter was gone again.

Amanda dared a slight smile. "That's wonderful."

Madge looked at her with tormented eyes. "James admitted he went to your apartment on his own last night, and not because you'd invited him. He—he's a proud man, my James, so it wasn't easy for him to say that you'd rejected him."

Not knowing what to say, Amanda simply waited, her hands folded in her lap, her diet cola untouched.

"He's agreed to come back home to California with me when he gets out of the hospital," Mrs. Brockman went on. "I don't know if that's a new start or what, but I do know this much—I love James. If there's any way we can begin again, well, I want a fighting chance."

"It's over between James and me," Amanda said gently. "It has been for months and months."

Mrs. Brockman's eyes held a flicker of hope. "You were telling the truth six months ago when

I confronted you in your office, weren't you? You honestly didn't know James was married."

Amanda sighed. "That's right. As soon as I found out, I broke it off."

"But you loved him, didn't you?"

Amanda felt a twinge of the pain that time and hard work and Jordan had finally healed. "Yes."

"Then why didn't you hold on? Why didn't you fight for him?"

"If he'd been my husband instead of yours, I would have," Amanda answered, reaching for her purse. She wasn't going to be able to choke down so much as a sip of that cola. "I'm not cut out to be the Other Woman, Mrs. Brockman. I want a man I don't have to share."

Madge Brockman smiled sadly as Amanda stood up. "Have you found one?"

"I hope so," Amanda answered. Then she laid a hand lightly on Mrs. Brockman's shoulder, just for a moment, before walking away.

Jordan arrived at seven o'clock on Friday night, looking slightly wan, his expensive suit wrinkled from the trip. "Hi, Mandy," he said, reaching out to gather her close.

Dressed for the island in blue jeans, walking boots and a heavy beige cable-knit sweater, Amanda went into his arms without hesitation.

"Hi," she answered, tilting her head back for his kiss.

He tasted her mouth before moving on to possess it entirely. "I don't suppose you're going to be merciful enough to tell me what you've decided," he said, sounding a little breathless, when the long kiss was over.

"About what?" Amanda asked with feigned innocence, and kissed the beard-stubbled underside of his chin. Of course she knew he wanted to know what the sleeping arrangements would be on the island that night.

Jordan laughed hoarsely and gave her a swat. "You know damn well 'about what'!" he lectured.

Despite the weariness she felt, Amanda grinned at him. "If you guess right, I'll tell you," she teased.

He studied her with tired, laughing, hungry eyes. "Okay, here's my guess. You're going to say you want to sleep in the guest room."

Amanda rocked back on her heels, resting against his hands, which were interwoven behind her, and said nothing.

"Well?" Jordan prodded.

"You guessed wrong," Amanda told him.

"Thank God," he groaned.

Amanda laughed. "Let's go—we'll miss the ferry."

Jordan's lips, warm and moist, touched hers. "We could just stay here—"

"No way, Mr. Richards," Amanda protested, pulling back. "You invited me to go away for the weekend and I want to *go away*."

"What about the cat?" Jordan reasoned as Gershwin jumped onto the back of an easy chair and meowed plaintively.

"My landlady is going to take care of him," Amanda said, pulling out of Jordan's embrace and picking up her suitcase and overnight case. "Here," she said, shoving the suitcase at him.

"I like a subtle woman," Jordan muttered, accepting it.

Soon they were leaving the heart of the city behind for West Seattle, where they caught the Southworth ferry. Once they were on board the enormous white boat, however, they remained in the car instead of going upstairs to the snack bar with most of the other passengers.

"I've missed you," Jordan said, leaning back in the seat, resting his hand on Amanda's upper thigh and gripping her fingers.

"And I've missed you," Amanda answered. They'd already run through all the small talk; Jordan had told her about his business trip and she'd detailed her hectic week. By tacit agreement, they hadn't discussed James's heart attack.

Jordan splayed the fingers of his left hand and ran them through his rumpled hair, then gave a heavy sigh. He moved his thumb soothingly over Amanda's knuckles. "Do you have any idea how much I want you?"

She lifted his hand to her mouth and kissed it. "How much?"

He chuckled. "Enough to wish this were a van instead of a sports car." Jordan turned in the seat and cupped Amanda's chin in his hand. "You're sure you're ready for this?" he asked gently.

Amanda nodded. "I'm sure. How about you?"

Jordan grinned. "I've been ready since I turned around and saw you standing in line behind me."

"You have not."

"Okay," he admitted, "it started after that, when you threw five bucks on the table to pay for your Chinese food. For just a moment, when you thought I was going to refuse it, you had blue fire in your eyes."

"And?"

"And I had this fantasy about the whole mall being deserted—except for us, of course. I made love to you right there on the table."

Amanda felt a hot shiver go through her. "Jordan?"

His lips were moving against hers. "Yes?"

"We're fogging up the windows. People will notice that."

He chuckled and drew back. "Maybe we should go upstairs and have some coffee or something, then."

She felt the rough texture of his cheek against her palm. "Then what kind of fantasies would you be having?"

"I'd probably start imagining that we were right here, alone in a dark car, with nobody around." Slowly he unbuttoned the front of her coat. "I suppose I'd picture myself touching you like this." He curved his fingers around her breast.

Even through the weight of her sweater and the lacy barrier of her bra, Amanda could feel his caress in every nerve. "Jordan."

He moved his hand beneath the sweater and then, to the accompaniment of a little gasp of surprised pleasure from Amanda, beneath the bra. Cupping her warm breast, he rolled the nipple gently between his fingers. "I'd be thinking about doing this, no doubt."

Amanda was squirming a little, and her breath was quickening. "Damn it, Jordan—this isn't funny. Someone could walk by!"

"Not likely," he murmured, touching his mouth to hers as he continued to fondle her.

Although she knew she should, Amanda couldn't bring herself to push his hand away. What he was doing felt too good. "S-someone might see—they'd think..."

Jordan bent his head to kiss the pulse point at the base of her throat. "They'd think we were necking. And they'd be right." Satisfied that he'd set one nipple to throbbing, he proceeded to attend the other. "Ummm. Where were you on prom night, lady?"

"Out with somebody like you," Amanda gasped breathlessly.

Jordan chuckled and continued nibbling at her throat. She felt the snap on her jeans pop, heard the faint whisper of the zipper. "Did he do this?"

The windows were definitely fogging up. "No..." Amanda moaned as he slid his fingers down her warm abdomen to find what they sought.

"Lift up your sweater," Jordan said. "I want to taste you."

Amanda whimpered a halfhearted protest even as she obeyed, but when she felt his mouth close over a distended nipple, she groaned out loud and entangled her fingers in his hair. In the meantime he continued the other delicious mischief, causing Amanda to fidget on the seat.

She ran her hands down his back, then up to his hair again in a frantic search for a place to touch him and make him feel what she was feeling. His name fell repeatedly from her lips in a breathless, senseless litany of passion.

Just as the ferry horn sounded, Amanda arched her back and cried out in release. Her body buckled over and over again against Jordan's hand before she sagged into the seat, temporarily soothed. Gradually her breathing steadied.

"Rat," she said when her good sense returned. She righted her bra and pulled her sweater down while Jordan zipped and snapped her jeans. Not two seconds after that, the first of the passengers returning from the upper deck walked past the car and waved.

Amanda's cheeks glowed as Jordan drove off the ferry minutes later.

"Relax, Mandy," he said, shoving a tape into the slot on the dashboard. The car filled with soft music. "I'm on your side, remember?"

She ran her tongue over her lips and turned in the seat to look at him. Her body was still quivering like a resonating string on some exotic instrument. "I'm not angry—just surprised. Nobody's ever been able to make me forget where I was."

"Good," Jordan replied, turning the Porsche onto a paved road lined with towering pine trees. "I'd be something less than thrilled if that was a regular thing with you."

Amanda gazed out the window for a moment, then looked back at Jordan. "Is it a regular thing with you?" she asked, almost in a whisper.

He looked at her, but she couldn't read his expression in the darkness. "There have been women since Becky, if that's what you mean. But if it'll make you feel better, none of them has ever had quite the same effect on me that you do. And I've never taken any of them to the island."

Amanda didn't know whether she felt better or not. She peered at his towering house as they pulled into the driveway, but all she could see was a shadowy shape and a lot of dark windows.

The garage door opened at the push of a button, and Jordan pulled in and got out, then turned on the lights before coming around to open Amanda's door for her. Gripping the handle of her suitcase in one hand, the other hand pressed to the small of her back, he escorted her through a side door and into a spacious, well-designed kitchen.

Amanda stopped when he set the suitcase down on the floor. "Did you live here with Becky?" she blurted. She'd known she wouldn't have the courage to ask if she waited too long.

"No," Jordan answered, taking the overnight case from her hand and setting it on the counter.

She shrugged out of her coat, avoiding his eyes. "Oh."

"Are you hungry or anything?" Jordan asked, glancing around the kitchen as though he expected it to be changed somehow from the last time he'd seen it.

"I could use a cup of coffee," Amanda admitted. "Maybe with a little brandy in it."

Jordan chuckled and disappeared with her coat. When he came back, he was minus his suit jacket and one hand was at his throat, loosening his tie. "The coffee maker's there on the counter," he said, pointing. "The other stuff is in the cupboard above it. Why don't you start the coffee brewing while I bring my stuff in from the car?"

It sounded like a reasonable idea to Amanda, and she was thankful for something to occupy her. What she and Jordan were about to do was as old as time, but she felt like the first virgin ever to be deflowered. She nodded and busily set about making coffee.

Jordan made one trip to the garage and then went upstairs. When he returned, he stood behind Amanda and put his arms around her. "Are you sure you want coffee? It's late, and that's the regular stuff."

His lips moved against her nape, and she couldn't help the tremor that went through her. "I guess not," she managed to say.

Without another word, Jordan lifted her into his arms and carried her through the dark house and up a set of stairs. The light was on in his spa-

cious bedroom, and Amanda murmured an ex-
clamation at the low-key luxury of the place.

The bed was enormous, and it faced a big-screen
TV equipped with a VCR and heaven-only-knows-
what other kinds of high-tech electronic equipment. One wall was made entirely of windows,
while another was lined with mirrors, and the gray
carpet was deep and plush.

Amanda glanced nervously at the mirrors and
saw her own wide eyes looking back at her.

Jordan kicked off his shoes, flung his tie aside
and vanished into the bathroom, whistling and
unbuttoning his shirt as he went. A few moments
later Amanda heard the sound of a shower running.

Quickly she scrambled off the bed and found
her suitcase, still feeling like a shy virgin. Suddenly the skimpy black nightgown she'd brought
along didn't look sturdy enough, so she helped
herself to a heavy terry-cloth robe from Jordan's
closet. After hastily stripping, she wrapped herself in the robe and tied the belt with a double
knot.

When Jordan came out sometime later, he was
wearing nothing but a towel around his waist. His
hair was blow-dried and combed back from his
face, and his eyes twinkled at Amanda when he
saw her sitting fitfully on the edge of the chair
farthest from the bed.

"Scared?" he asked, approaching her and pulling her gently to her feet.

"Of course not," Amanda lied. The truth was, she was terrified.

Jordan undid the double knot at her waist as though it were nothing. "I guess I should have invited you to share my shower," he said, his voice a leisurely rumble.

"I had one at home," Amanda was quick to point out.

He opened the robe, laid it aside and looked at her, slowly and thoroughly, before meeting her eyes again. His lips quirked. "You're awfully nervous, considering how mad you were when I wouldn't make love to you last week."

Amanda moved to close the robe, but Jordan grasped her wrists and stopped her. He subjected her to another lingering assessment before pushing the garment off her shoulders with warm, gentle hands. It fell silently to the floor.

"We—we could turn the light out," she dared to suggest as Jordan lifted her again and carried her back to the bed.

"We could," he agreed, stretching out beside her, "but we're not going to."

He'd shaved, and his face was smooth and fragrant. He took her mouth and mastered it skillfully, leaving Amanda dizzy and disoriented when he drew away.

Tenderly he turned Amanda's head so that she was facing the mirrors, and a moan lodged in her throat when she saw him move his hand toward her breast.

"Jordan," she whispered.

"Shhh," he murmured against the tingling flesh of her neck, and Amanda was quiet, her eyes widening as she watched her conquering begin.

# 6

The dark blue velour bedspread felt incredibly soft against Amanda's bare skin, and she forgot the mirrored wall and even the lights as Jordan kissed and caressed her. Although she tried, she couldn't hold back the soft moans that escaped her, or the whispered pleas for release.

But Jordan would not be hurried. "All in good time, Mandy," he assured her, his mouth at her throat. "All in good time. Just relax."

"Relax?" Amanda gave a rueful semihysterical chuckle at the word. "Now? Are you crazy?"

He trailed his lips down over her collarbone, over the plump rounding of one breast. "Ummm-hmm," he said just before he took her nipple into his mouth. In the meantime he was stroking the tender skin on the insides of Amanda's thighs.

"Stop teasing me," she whimpered, moving her hands through his hair and over the muscular sleekness of his back.

"Never," he paused long enough to say. He left off tormenting Amanda to reach for a pillow, which he deftly tucked underneath her bottom. And then he caressed her in earnest.

Amanda was frantic. Jordan had been subjecting her to various kinds of foreplay for a week, and she simply couldn't wait any longer for gratification. Her body demanded it.

"Jordan," she pleaded, half-blind with the need of him, "*now*. Oh, please—"

She felt him part her legs, then come to rest between them. "Mandy," he rasped like a man being consumed by invisible fire. In one fierce, beautiful thrust, he was a part of her, but then he lay very still. "Mandy, open your eyes and look at me."

She obeyed, but she could barely focus on his features because she was caught up in a whirlwind of sensation. The pillow raised her to him like a pagan offering, and her body was still reacting to the single stroke he'd allowed her. "Jordan," she pleaded, and all her desperation, all her need, echoed in the name.

He kissed her thoroughly, his tongue staking the same claim that the other part of his body was making on her. Finally he began to move upon her, slowly at first, making her ask for every motion of his powerful hips, but as Amanda's passion heated, so did his own. Soon they were parting and coming together again in a wild, primitive rhythm.

Amanda was the first to scale the peak, and the splintering explosion in her senses was everything she'd hoped it would be. Her body arched like a bow with the string drawn tight, and her cries of surrender echoed off the walls.

Jordan was more restrained, but Amanda saw a panorama of emotions crossed his face as he gave himself up to her in a series of short, frenzied thrusts.

They lay on their sides, facing each other, legs still entwined, for long minutes after their lovemaking had ended.

Jordan gave a raspy chuckle.

"What's funny?" Amanda asked softly, winding a tendril of his rich brown hair around one finger.

"I was just thinking of the first time I saw you. You were bored with waiting in line, so you struck up a conversation. I wondered if you were a member of some weird religious sect."

Amanda gave him a playful punch in the chest.

He laughed and leaned over to kiss her. "Let's go down to the kitchen," he said when it was over. "I'm starving."

Jordan rose off the bed and retrieved the yellow bathrobe from the floor, tossing it to Amanda. He took a hooded one of striped silk from the closet and put that on. Together, they went downstairs.

Jordan plundered the cupboards, while Amanda perched on a stool, watching him and sipping a cup of the coffee she'd made earlier. He finally decided on popcorn and thrust a bag into the microwave.

"This is a great house," Amanda said as the oven's motor began to whir. "What I've seen of it, anyway."

Jordan was busy digging through another cupboard for a serving bowl that suited him. "Thanks."

"And it's pretty big." Saying those words gave Amanda the same sense of breathless anticipation she would have felt if she'd walked outside with the intention of plunging a toe into the frigid sound.

He set a red bowl on the counter with a thump, and the grin he gave her was tinged with exasperation. "Big enough for a couple of kids, I suppose," he said.

Amanda shrugged and lifted her eyebrows. "Seems like you could fit Jessica and Lisa in here somewhere."

The popcorn was snapping like muted gunfire inside its colorful paper bag. For just a moment, Jordan's eyes snapped, too. "We've been over that, Amanda," he said.

She took another sip of her coffee. "Okay. I was just wondering why you'd want a house like this when you live all alone."

The bell on the microwave chimed, and Jordan took the popcorn out, carefully opened the bag and dumped the contents into the bowl. The fragrance filled the kitchen, causing Amanda to decide she was hungry, after all.

"Jordan?" she prompted when he didn't reply.

He picked up a kernel and tossed it at her. "How about cooling it with the questions I can't answer?"

Amanda sighed and wriggled off the stool. "I'm sorry," she said. "Your living arrangements are none of my business, anyway."

Jordan didn't counter that statement. He simply took up the bowl and started back through the house and up the stairs. Amanda had no choice but to follow.

Returning to the bed, they settled themselves under the covers, with pillows at their backs, the popcorn between them, and Jordan switched on the gigantic TV screen.

The news was on. "I'm not in the mood to be depressed," Jordan said, working the remote control device with his thumb until a cable channel came on.

Amanda settled against his shoulder and crunched thoughtfully on a mouthful of popcorn. "I've seen this movie before," she said. "It's good."

Jordan slipped an arm around her and plunged the opposite hand into the bowl. "I'll take your word for it."

Images flickered across the screen, the popcorn diminished until there were only yellow kernels in the bottom of the bowl and the moon rose high and beautiful beyond the wall of windows. Amanda sighed and closed her eyes, feeling warm and contented.

The next thing she knew, it was morning, and Jordan was lying beside her, propped up on one elbow, smiling. "Hi," he said. He'd showered, and his breath smelled of mint toothpaste.

Amanda was well aware she hadn't and hers didn't. "Hi," she responded, speaking into the covers.

Jordan laughed and kissed her forehead. "Breakfast in twenty minutes," he said, and then he rose off the bed and walked away, wearing only a pair of jeans.

The moment he was gone, Amanda dashed to the bathroom. When he returned in the prescribed twenty minutes, he was carrying a tray and Amanda was sitting cross-legged in the middle of the bed. She'd exchanged Jordan's robe for a short nightgown of turquoise silk, and she grinned when she saw the tray in his hands.

"Room service! I'm impressed, Mr. Richards."

He set the food tray carefully in her lap, and Amanda's stomach rumbled in anticipation as she looked under various lids, finding sliced banana, toast, orange juice and two slices of crisp bacon. "Our services are *très* expensive, *madame*," he teased in a very good French accent.

"Put it on my credit card," Amanda bantered back, and picked up a slice of bacon and bit into it.

Jordan chuckled, still playing the Frenchman. "Oh, but *madame*, this we cannot do." He reached out to touch the tip of her right breast with his index finger, making the nipple turn button-hard beneath its covering of silk. "Zee policy is strictly cash and carry."

Amanda's eyes were sparkling as she widened them in mock horror. "We have a terrible problem then, *monsieur*, for I haven't a franc to my name. Not a single, solitary one!"

"This is a true pity," Jordan continued, laying a light, exploratory finger to Amanda's knee and drawing it slowly down to her ankle. "I am afraid you cannot leave this room until you have made proper restitution."

Amanda ate in silence for a time, while Jordan lingered, watching her with mischievous expectancy in his eyes. "Aren't you going to eat?" she asked, forgetting the game for a moment, and she went red the instant the words were out of her mouth.

Jordan chuckled, took the tray from her lap and set it aside. "About the price of your room, *madame*. Some agreement must be reached."

Recovered from her earlier embarrassment, Amanda slipped her arms around Jordan's neck and kissed him softly on the lips. "I'm sure we can work out something to our mutual satisfaction, *monsieur*."

He drew the silk nightgown gently over her head and tossed it away. *"Oui,"* he answered, laying a hand to her bare thigh even as he pressed her back onto the pillows.

Amanda groaned as he moved his hand from her thigh to her stomach, and when instinct caused her to draw up her knees, he claimed her with a finger in a sudden motion of his hand.

The sensation was exquisite, and Amanda arched her neck, her eyes drifting closed as Jordan choreographed a dance for her eager body. She groaned as Jordan's tongue tamed a pulsing nipple.

"Of course," he told her in that same accented English, "the customer, she must always have satisfaction first."

Only moments later, Amanda was caught in the throes of a climax that caused her to thrash on the bed and call Jordan's name even as she clutched blindly at his shoulders.

"Easy," he told her, moving his warm lips against her neck. "Nice and easy."

Amanda sagged back to the mattress, her breath coming in fevered gasps, her eyes smoldering as she watched Jordan slip out of his jeans and poise himself above her. "No more waiting," she said. "I want you, Jordan."

He gave her only a portion of his magnificence at first, but then, when she traced the circumference of each of his nipples with a fingertip, he gave a low growl and plunged into her in earnest. And the whole splendid rite began all over again.

"A Christmas tree?" Amanda echoed, standing in the middle of Jordan's living room with its high, beamed ceilings and breathtaking view of the mountains and Puget Sound. She was wearing jeans, sneakers and a sweatshirt, like Jordan, and there was a cozy fire snapping on the raised hearth.

"Is that so strange?" Jordan asked. "After all, it is December."

Amanda assessed the towering tinted glass window that let in the view. "It would be a shame to cover that up," she said.

Jordan pinched her cheek. "Thank you, Ebenezer Scrooge," he teased. Then he widened his eyes at her. "What is it with you and Christmas, anyway?"

With a sigh, Amanda collapsed into a cushy chair upholstered in dark blue brushed cotton, her arms folded. "I guess I'd like to let it just sort of slip past unnoticed."

"Fat chance," Jordan replied, perching on the arm of her chair. "It's everywhere."

"Yeah," Amanda said, lowering her eyes.

He put a finger under her chin and lifted. "What is it, Mandy?"

She tried to smile. "My dad left at Christmas," she admitted, her voice small as she momentarily became a little girl again.

"Ouch," Jordan whispered, pulling her to her feet. Then he sank into the chair and drew Amanda onto his lap. "That was a dirty trick."

"You don't know the half of it," Amanda reflected, staring out at mountains she didn't really see. "We never heard another word from him, ever. He didn't even take his presents."

Jordan pressed Amanda's head against his shoulder. "Know what?" he asked softly. "Hating Christmas isn't going to change what happened.''

She lifted her head so that she could look into Jordan's eyes. "It's the hardest time of the year when you've lost somebody you loved.''

He kissed her forehead. "Believe me, Mandy, I know that. The first year after Becky died, Jessie asked me to write a letter to Santa Claus for her. She wanted him to bring her mother back.''

Amanda smoothed the hair at Jordan's temple, even though it wasn't rumpled. "What did you do?''

"My first impulse was to get falling-down drunk and stay that way until spring." He sighed. "I didn't, of course. With some help from my sister, I explained to Jessie that even Santa couldn't pull off anything that big. It was tough, but we all got through it.''

"Don't you miss them?" Amanda dared to ask, her voice barely more than a breath. "Jessica and Lisa, I mean?''

"Every day of my life," Jordan replied, "but I've got to think about what's best for them." His tone said the conversation was over, and so did his action. He got out of the chair, propelling Amanda to her feet in the process. "Let's go cut a Christmas tree.''

Amanda smiled. "I haven't done that since I was still at home. My stepdad used to take my sister and me along every year—we drove all the way to Issaquah.''

"So," Jordan teased with a light in his eyes, "your memories of Christmas aren't all bad."

Recalling how hard Bob had tried to make up not only for Marion's loss, but the girls', as well, Amanda had a warm feeling. "You're right," she admitted.

Jordan squinted at her and twisted the end of an imaginary mustache. This time his accent was Viennese, and he was, according to Amanda's best guess, Sigmund Freud. "Absolutely of course I am right," he said.

And then he pulled Amanda close and kissed her soundly, and she found herself wanting to go back upstairs.

That wasn't in the cards, however. Jordan had decided to cut down a Christmas tree, and his purpose was evidently unshakable. They put on coats, climbed into the small, late-model pickup truck parked beside the Porsche and sped off toward the tree farm.

Slogging up and down the rows of Christmas trees while the attendant walked behind them with a chain saw at the ready, Amanda actually felt festive. The piney smell was pungent, the air crisp, the sky painfully blue.

"How about this one?" Jordan said, pausing to inspect a twelve-footer.

Amanda looked at him in bewilderment. "What about it?"

Jordan gave her a wry glance. "Do you like it?" he asked patiently.

Amanda couldn't think why it mattered whether she liked the tree or not, but she nodded. "It's beautiful."

"We'll take this one," Jordan told the attendant.

They stood back while the man in the plaid woolen coat and blue overalls felled the tree, and followed when he dragged it off toward the truck.

By the time the tree had been paid for and tied down in the back of Jordan's truck, it was noon and Amanda was famished.

Jordan favored her with a sidelong grin when they were seated in the cab. "Hungry?"

"How do you always know?" Amanda demanded, half surprised and half exasperated. A person couldn't have a private thought around this man.

"I'm psychic," Jordan teased, starting the engine. "Of course, the fact that you haven't eaten in four hours and your stomach is rumbling helped me come to the conclusion. How does seafood sound?"

"Wonderful," Amanda replied. The scent of the tree was on her clothes and Jordan's, and she loved its pungency.

They drove to a café overlooking the water and took a table next to a window, where they could see a ferry passing, along with the occasional intrepid sailboat and a number of other small vessels. Jordan flirted with the middle-aged waitress, who obviously knew him and gave Amanda a kindly assessment with heavily made-up eyes.

"So, Jordan Richards," the older woman teased, "you've been stepping out on me."

Jordan grinned. "Sorry, Wanda."

Wanda swatted him on the shoulder with a plastic-covered menu. "I'm always the last to know," she said. Her eyes came back to Amanda again. "Since Jordan doesn't have enough manners to introduce us, we'll just have to handle the job ourselves. My name's Wanda Carson."

Amanda smiled and held out her hand. "Amanda Scott," she replied.

After shaking Amanda's hand, Wanda laid the menus down and said, "We got a real good special today. It's baked chicken with rice."

Jordan ordered the special, perhaps to atone for 'stepping out on' Wanda, but Amanda had her heart set on seafood, so she ordered deep-fried prawns and French fries.

Amanda couldn't remember ever enjoying a meal more than she did that one, but honesty would have forced her to admit it was not the food but the company that made it special.

On the way back to Jordan's house, they stopped at a variety store, which was crowded with shopping carts and people, and bought an enormous tree stand, strings of lights, colorful glass ornaments and tinsel. "I gave away the stuff Becky and I had," he admitted offhandedly while they waited in line to pay.

A bittersweet pang squeezed Amanda's heart at the thought, but she only smiled.

They spent a good hour just dragging the massive tree inside the house and setting it up. It fell over repeatedly, and Jordan finally had to put hooks in the wall and tie it in place. It towered to the ceiling, every needle of its fresh, green branches filling the room with perfume.

"It's beautiful," Amanda vowed, resting her hands on her hips.

Jordan was bringing a high stepladder in from the garage. "So are you," he told her, setting the ladder up beside the tree. "In fact, why don't you come over here?"

Amanda laughed and shook her head. "No thanks. This fly knows a spider when she sees one."

Assuming a pretend glower, Jordan stomped over to Amanda, put his fingers against her ribs and tickled her until she toppled onto the couch, shrieking with laughter.

Then he pinned her down with his body and stretched her arms far above her head. "Hello, fly," he said, his eyes twinkling as he placed his mouth on hers.

"Hello, spider," Amanda responded, her lips touching his. Just as the piney scent of the tree pervaded the house, Jordan's closeness permeated her senses.

Things might have progressed from there if the telephone hadn't rung, but it did, and Jordan reached over Amanda's head to grasp the receiver. There was a note of impatience in his voice when he answered, but his expression changed completely when the caller spoke.

He sat up on the edge of the couch, Amanda apparently forgotten. "Hi, Jessie. I'm fine, honey. How are you?"

Amanda suddenly felt like an eavesdropper. She got up from the couch and tiptoed out of the living room and up the stairs. She was pacing back and forth across the bedroom, when she noticed an overturned photograph on the bedside table.

An ache twisted in the pit of her stomach as she walked over, grasped the photograph and set it upright. A beautiful dark-haired woman smiled at her from the picture, her eyes full of love and laughter.

"Hello, Becky," Amanda whispered sadly, recalling the white stripe on Jordan's finger where his wedding band had been.

Becky seemed to regard her with kind understanding.

Amanda set the photo carefully back on the bedside table and stood up. A fathomless sorrow filled her; she felt as though she'd made love to another woman's husband. But this time she'd known what she was doing.

Turning her back on the picture, Amanda found her suitcase and her overnighter and packed them both. She was just snapping the catches on the suitcase, when the door opened and Jordan came in.

His gaze shifted from Amanda to the photograph and back again. "Is this about the picture?" he asked quietly.

Amanda lowered her head. "I'm not sure."

"Not good enough, Mandy." Jordan's voice was husky. "Until ten minutes ago when my daughters called, everything was okay. Then you came up here and saw the picture, and you packed your clothes."

She made herself look at him, and it hurt that he lingered in the doorway instead of crossing the room to take her into his arms. "I guess I feel like this is her house and you're her husband. It's kind of like being the other woman all over again."

"That's crazy."

Amanda shook her head. "No, it isn't. Look at your left hand, Jordan. You can still see where the wedding band was. When did you take it off? Two weeks ago? Last month?"

Jordan folded his arms. "What does it matter when I took it off? The point is, I'm not wearing it anymore. And as for the picture, I just forgot to put it away, that's all."

"The night we had dinner at my place, you told me I wasn't ready for a relationship. I think maybe *you're* the one who isn't ready, Jordan."

He sprang away from the door frame, strode across the room and took the suitcase and overnighter from Amanda's hands, tossing them aside with a clatter. "Remember me? I'm the guy whose mind you blew in that bed over there," he bit out. "Damn it, have you forgotten the way it was with us?"

"That isn't the issue!" Amanda cried, frustrated and confused.

"Isn't it?" Jordan asked, clasping her wrists in his hands and wrenching her close to him. "You're scared, Amanda, so you're looking for an excuse to make a quick exit. That way you won't have to face what's really happening here."

Amanda swallowed hard. "What *is* happening here?" she asked miserably.

Jordan withdrew from her, albeit reluctantly, except for the grip he'd taken on her hand. "I don't know exactly," he confessed, calmer now. "But I think we'd damn well better find out, don't you?"

At Amanda's nod, he led her out of the bedroom and down the stairs again. She sank despondently into an easy chair while he built up the fire on the hearth.

"I don't want to be the other woman, Jordan," she said when he turned to face her.

He crossed the room, knelt in front of her and placed one of her blue-jeaned legs over each arm of the chair, setting her afire all over again as he stroked the insides of her thighs. "You're the *only* woman," he answered, and he nipped at one of her nipples through the bra and sweatshirt that covered it. "Show me your breasts, Mandy."

It was a measure of her obsession with him that she pulled up her sweatshirt and unfastened the front catch on her bra so that she spilled out into full view. He grasped her knees, holding them up on the arms of the chair as he leaned forward to tease one nipple with his tongue.

Amanda remembered that there was somebody else in Jordan's life, but she couldn't remember a face or a name. Perspiration glowed on her upper lip as Jordan took his pleasure at her breasts, moving his right hand from one knee to the other, slowly following an erotic path.

Finally, when Amanda was half-delirious with wanting, he kissed his way down over her belly and lightly bit her through the denim at the cross-roads of her thighs.

Amanda moaned helplessly and moved to close her legs, and Jordan allowed that, but only long enough to unsnap her jeans and dispose of them, along with her panties and shoes. Then he put her knees back into their original position, opened his own jeans and took her in a powerful, possessive thrust so pleasurable that she nearly fainted.

She longed to embrace Jordan with her legs, as well as her arms, but he didn't permit it. It was a battle of sorts, but Amanda couldn't be sure who was the loser, since every lunge Jordan made wrung a cry of delight from her throat.

Her climax made her give a long, low scream as she pressed her head into the chair's back. Jordan, both hands still holding her knees, uttered a desolate groan as his body convulsed and he spilled himself into Amanda.

Once the gasping aftermath was over and Amanda's breathing and heart rate had gone back to normal, she was angry. Jordan hadn't forced her, but he had turned her own body against her, and that was a power no one had ever had over Amanda before.

She moved to fasten her bra, but Jordan, still breathing hard, his eyes flashing with challenge, interrupted the action and took her tingling breasts gently but firmly into his hands. "We're not through, Amanda," he ground out.

"The hell we aren't!" she sputtered.

Keeping his hands where they were, he turned his head and lightly kissed the back of her knee.

Amanda trembled. "Damn it, Jordan . . ."

He moved his lips along her inner thigh, leaving a trail of fire behind them, and slid one of his hands down to rest on her lower abdomen, finding the hidden plum and making a small circle around it with the pad of his thumb. "Yes?" he answered at his leisure.

A whimper escaped Amanda, and Jordan chuckled at the sound, still working his lethal magic. "You were saying?" he prompted huskily.

Amanda reached backward to grasp the top of the chair, fearing she would fly away like a rocket if she didn't. "We're n-not through," she concluded.

Her reward was another baptism in sweet fire, and it made a believer out of her through and through.

The next day was cold and pristinely beautiful, and Jordan and Amanda decided to leave the tree undecorated and take a drive around the island. That was when Amanda saw the house.

It stood between Jordan's place and the ferry terminal, and she couldn't imagine why she hadn't noticed it before. It was white with green shutters, and very Victorian, and there was even a lighthouse within walking distance. Best of all a For Sale sign stood in the yard, swinging slowly in the salty breeze.

"Jordan, stop!" Amanda cried, barely able to restrain herself from reaching out and grasping the steering wheel.

After giving her one half-amused, half-bewildered look, Jordan steered the truck onto the rocky, rutted driveway leading past a tumble-down mailbox and a few discarded tires and empty rabbit pens.

Amanda was out of the truck a moment after they came to a jolting halt.

# 7

The grass in the yard was overgrown, and the outside of the building needed paint, but neither of these facts dampened Amanda's enthusiasm. She hurried around the back of the house and found a screened porch that ran the full length of the place. On the upper floor there were lots of windows, providing an unobstructed view of the water and the mountains.

It was the perfect place for a bed and breakfast, and Amanda felt a thrill of excitement race through her blood.

A moment later, though, as Jordan caught up to her, her spirits plummeted. The place had obviously been neglected for a long time and would cost far more than she had to spend. People were willing to pay a premium price for waterfront property.

"I could help you," Jordan suggested, reading her mind.

Amanda quickly shook her head. A personal loan could poison their relationship if things went wrong later on, and besides, she wanted the accomplishment to be her own.

After they'd walked around the house and looked into the windows, Amanda wrote down the name of the real estate company and the phone number, tucking the information into her purse.

She could hardly wait to get to a telephone, and Jordan, discerning this, headed straight for the café where Wanda worked. While he chatted with the waitress and ordered clubhouse sandwiches, Amanda dialed the real estate agency's number and got an answering machine. She left her name and her numbers for home and work in Seattle and returned to the table.

"No luck?" Jordan asked as she sat down across from him in the booth and reached for the cup of coffee he'd ordered for her.

"They'll get in touch," Amanda answered with a little shrug. "I don't know why I'm so excited. I probably won't be able to afford the place, anyway."

Jordan's eyes twinkled as he looked at her. "That was a negative thing to say," he scolded. "You're not going to get anywhere in life if you don't believe in yourself."

"Thank you, Norman Vincent Peale," Amanda said somewhat irritably as she wriggled out of her coat and set it aside. "Just because you could probably write a check for the place on the spot doesn't mean I'd be able to."

The clubhouse sandwiches arrived, and Jordan picked up a potato chip and crunched it between his teeth. "Okay, so I have a knack with money. I should have—it's my business. And I don't understand why you won't let me help."

"I have my reasons, Jordan."

"Like what?"

Amanda shrugged. "Suppose in two days or two weeks we decide we don't want to see each other anymore. If I owed you a big chunk of money, things could get pretty sticky."

Jordan shook his head. "That's just an excuse, Mandy. People borrow money to start businesses every day of the week."

In the short time they'd known each other, Amanda had to admit that Jordan had learned to read her well. "I want it to be mine," she confessed. "Is that too much to ask?"

"Nope," Jordan replied good-naturedly, and after that they dropped the subject and talked of other things.

They spent the rest of the afternoon exploring the beach fronting the property Amanda wanted to buy, and the time sped by. Too soon the weekend was over and Jordan was putting her suitcase and overnighter in the back of the Porsche.

Even the prospect of separation was difficult for Amanda. "How about having dinner at my place before you come back?" she asked somewhat shyly as Jordan pushed the button to turn on the answering machine in his study.

He smiled at her. "Smooth talker," he teased.

Amanda barely stopped herself from suggesting that he bring fresh clothes and a toothbrush, as well. All her life she'd been a patient, methodical person, but where this man was concerned, she had a dangerous tendency to be impulsive. She trembled a little when Jordan kissed her, and devoutly hoped he hadn't noticed.

During the ferry ride back to Seattle, they drank coffee in the snack bar, and when they reached the city, Amanda asked Jordan to stop at a supermarket. She bought chicken, fresh corn and potatoes.

Gershwin greeted them with a mournful meow when they entered Amanda's apartment. Appeasing his pique was easy, though; Jordan simply opened a can of cat food and set it on the floor for him.

Amanda was busy cutting up the chicken and washing the corn, so Jordan wandered back into the living room and used the log left from his last visit to start a fire on the hearth.

"We forgot to decorate your tree," Amanda said when he returned to the kitchenette to lean against the counter, watching her put floured chicken pieces into a hot skillet.

"It'll keep," Jordan answered. When she'd finished putting the chicken on to brown, he took her into his arms. "Mandy, Karen's bringing the girls to Seattle Friday night. They're going to spend two weeks with me."

Amanda was pleased, but a little puzzled that he'd waited until now to mention it. "That's great. I guess you found that out when the kids called."

He nodded.

"Why didn't you tell me?"

Jordan shrugged. "If you recall, we were a little busy after that phone call," he pointed out. "And then I was trying to work out how to ask you to spend next weekend on the island with us."

Amanda broke away long enough to turn the chicken pieces and put the corn on to boil. "I don't think that would be a very good idea, Jordan," she finally said, looking back at him over her shoulder. "After all, we aren't married, and we don't want to confuse the kids."

"How could we confuse them? They're not teenagers, Amanda. They're too small to understand about sex."

Amanda shook her head. "Kids know something is going on, whether they understand what it is or not. They sense emotional undercurrents, Jordan, and I don't want to get off on the wrong foot with them." She turned down the heat under the chicken and covered it with a lid. "Now how about a glass of wine?"

Jordan nodded his assent, but he looked distracted. After uncorking the bottle and pouring a glass for himself and for Amanda, he wandered into the living room.

Amanda followed, perching on the arm of the sofa while he stood at the window, watching the city lights.

"Come on, Jordan," she urged gently. "'Fess up. You're scared, aren't you? When was the last time you were responsible for your kids for two weeks straight?"

There was a hint of anger in his eyes when he turned to look at her. "I've been 'responsible' for them since they were born, Amanda."

"Maybe so," she retorted quietly, "but somebody else did the nitty-gritty stuff—first Becky, then your sister. You don't have any idea how to really take care of your daughters, do you?"

Jordan was offended initially, but then his ire gave way to a sort of indignant resignation. "Okay," he admitted, "you've got me. I wanted you to spend next weekend with us because I need moral support."

Amanda went back to the kitchen for plates and silverware, then began to set the small, round table in the living room. "You know my phone number," she said. "If you want moral support, you can call me. But you don't need somebody else in the way when you're bonding with your kids, Jordan."

"Bonding? Hell, you've been reading too many pop psychology books."

"You have a right to your opinion," Amanda responded, "but I'm not going to be there to act as a buffer. You're on your own with this one, buddy."

Jordan gave her an irate look, but then his expression softened and he took her in his arms. "Maybe I can't change your mind," he told her huskily, "but I can sure as hell let you know what you'll be missing."

Amanda pushed him away. "The chicken will burn."

Jordan chuckled. "Okay, Mandy, you win. For now."

Twenty minutes later they sat down to a dinner of fried chicken, corn on the cob, mashed potatoes and gravy. Amanda's portable TV set was turned to the evening news, and the ambience of the evening was quietly domestic.

When they were through eating, Amanda began clearing the table, only to have Jordan stop her by slipping his arms around her waist from behind. "Aren't you forgetting something?" he asked, his voice a low rumble as he bent his head to kiss her nape and sent a jagged thrill swirling through her system.

"W-what?" Amanda asked, already a little breathless.

Jordan slid his hands up beneath her shirt to cup the undersides of her breasts. "Dessert," he answered.

Amanda was trembling. "Jordan, the food—"

"The food will still be here when we're through."

"No, it won't," Amanda argued, following her protest with a little moan as Jordan unfastened her bra and rubbed her nipples to attention with the sides of his thumbs. "G-Gershwin will eat it."

His lips were on her nape again. "Who cares?"

Amanda realized that she didn't. She turned in Jordan's embrace and tilted her head back for his kiss.

While taming her mouth, he grasped her hips in his hands and pressed her close, making her feel his size and power.

She was dazed when he drew back, pliant when he steered her toward the bedroom and closed the door behind them.

The small room was shadowy, the bed neatly made. Jordan set Amanda on the edge of the mattress and knelt to slowly untie her shoes and roll down her socks. For a time he caressed her feet, one by one, and Amanda was surprised at the sensual pleasure such a simple act could evoke.

When she was tingling from head to foot, he rose and pulled her shirt off over her head, then smoothed away the bra he'd already opened. He pressed Amanda onto her back to unsnap her jeans and remove them and her panties, and she didn't make a move to stop him. All she could do was sigh.

After the last of her garments was tossed away, Jordan began removing his own clothes. They joined Amanda's in a pile on the floor.

"Jordan," Amanda whispered, entwining her fingers in his hair as he stretched out beside her, "don't make me wait. Please."

He gave her a nibbling kiss. "So impatient," he scolded sleepily, trailing his lips down over her chin to her neck. "Lovemaking takes time, Mandy. Especially if it's good."

Amanda remembered their session in Jordan's living room the day before. It had been fast and ferocious, and if it had been any better, it would have killed her. She moaned as Jordan made a slow, silken circle on her belly with his hand. "I can only stand so much pleasure!" she whimpered in a lame protest.

Jordan chuckled. "We're going to have to raise your tolerance," he said.

* * *

Two hours later, when both Jordan and Amanda were showered and dressed and the table had been cleared, he reached for his jacket and shrugged into it. Amanda had to fight back tears when he kissed her, as well as pleas for him to spend the night. On a practical, rational level, she knew they both needed to let things cool down a little so they could get some perspective.

But when she'd closed the door behind Jordan, Amanda rested her forehead against it for a long moment and bit down hard on her lower lip. It was all she could do not to run out into the hallway and call him back.

Slowly she turned from the door and went about her usual Sunday night routine, choosing the outfits she would wear to work during the coming week, manicuring her nails and watching a mystery program on TV.

The bed was rumpled, and it still smelled of Jordan's cologne and their fevered lovemaking. Forlornly Amanda remade it and crawled under the covers, the small TV she kept in her room turned to her favorite show.

Two minutes after that week's victim had been done in, the telephone rang. Hoping for a call from the real estate agent or from Jordan, Amanda reached for the receiver on her bedside table and answered on the second ring.

"Amanda?"

The voice was Eunice's, and she sounded as though she'd been crying for a week.

Amanda spoke gently to her sister, because they'd always been close. "Hi, kid," she said, for she was the older of the two and Eunice had been "kid" since she was born. "What's the problem?"

"It's Jim," Eunice sobbed.

*Now there's a real surprise,* Amanda thought ruefully while she waited for her sister to recover herself.

"There's been someone else the whole time," Eunice wept, making a valiant, sniffling attempt to get a hold on herself.

Amanda was painfully reminded of what Madge Brockman had gone through because of her. "Are you sure?" she asked gently.

"She called this afternoon," Eunice said. "She said if Jim wouldn't tell me, she would. He's moved in with her!"

For a moment Amanda knew a pure, white-hot rage entirely directed at her soon-to-be ex-brother-in-law. Since her anger wouldn't help Eunice in any way, she counted to herself until the worst of it had passed. "Honey, this doesn't look like something you can change. And that means you have to accept it."

Eunice was quiet for almost a minute. "I guess you're right," she admitted softly. "I'll try, Amanda."

"I know you will," Amanda replied, wishing she could be nearer to her sister to lend moral support.

"Mom tells me you've met a guy." Eunice snuffled. "That's really great, Mand. What's he like?"

Amanda remembered making love with Jordan on the very bed she was lying in, and a wave of heat rolled over her. She also remembered the photograph of Becky and the white strip of skin on Jordan's left hand ring finger. "He's moderately terrific," she answered demurely.

Eunice laughed, and it was a good sound to hear. "Maybe I can meet him when I come home next week."

"I'd like that," Amanda replied. "And I'm glad you're coming home. How long can you stay?"

"Perhaps forever," Eunice replied, sounding blue again. "Everywhere I turn here, there's another reminder of Jim staring me in the face."

Amanda spoke gently. "Don't misunderstand me, sis, because I'd love for you to live in Seattle again, but I hope you realize you can't run away from your problems. You'll still have to find a way to work them out."

"That might be easier with you and Mom and Bob nearby," Eunice said quietly.

"You know we'll help in any way we can," Amanda assured her.

"Yeah, I know. It means the world to know you're there for me, Mand—you and Mom and Daddy Bob. But listen, I'll get off the line now because I know you're probably trying to watch that murder show you like so much. See you next week."

Amanda smiled. "You just try and avoid it, kid."

After that, the two sisters said their goodbyes and hung up. Amanda, having lost track of her TV show, switched off the set and the lamp on her bedside table and wriggled down between the covers.

How empty the bed seemed without Jordan sprawled out beside her, taking more than his share of the space.

Two days passed before Amanda saw Jordan again; they met for lunch in a hotel restaurant.

"Did you ever hear from the real estate agent?" Jordan asked, drawing back Amanda's chair for her.

She sank into it, inordinately relieved just to be with him again. She wondered, with a chill, if she wasn't letting herself in for a major bruise to the soul somewhere down the line. "She called me at work yesterday. The down payment is five times what I have in the bank."

Jordan sat down across from her and reached out for her hand, which she willingly gave. "Mandy, I can lend you the money with no problem."

"You must be loaded," Amanda teased, having no intention of accepting, "if you can make an offer like that without even knowing how much is involved."

He grinned one of his melting grins. "I confess—I called the agency and asked."

Amanda shook out her napkin and placed it neatly on her lap. It was time to change the subject. "Who's going to take care of the kids while you're working?" she asked.

"Much to the consternation of Striner and Striner," said Jordan, "I'm taking two weeks off. I figure I'm going to need all my wits about me."

Amanda laughed. "No doubt about that."

Jordan leaned forward in his chair with a look of mock reprimand on his face. "I'll thank you to extend a little sympathy, here, Ms. Scott. You're looking at a man who has no idea how to take care of two little girls."

"They need to eat three times a day, Jordan," Amanda pointed out with teasing patience, "and it's a good idea if they have a bath at night, followed by about eight hours of sleep. Beyond that, they mainly just need to know they're loved."

Jordan was turning his table knife from end to end. "You're sure you won't come out for the weekend?"

"My sister is arriving on Friday night—in pieces, from the sounds of things."

"Ah," Jordan answered as a waiter brought menus and filled their water glasses. "The recipient of *Gathering Up the Pieces*, the pop psychology book of the decade. I'm sorry to hear things haven't improved for her."

Amanda sighed. "They've gone from bad to worse, actually," she replied. "But there's hope. Eunice is intelligent, and she's attractive, too. She'll work through this."

"Maybe she could work through the first part of it—say next Saturday and Sunday—without you?"

Amanda shook her head as she opened her menu. "Don't you ever give up?"

"Never," Jordan replied. "It's my credo—keep bugging them until they give in to shut you up."

Amanda laughed. "Such sage advice."

They made their selections and placed their orders before the conversation continued. Jordan reached out and took Amanda's hand again when the waiter was gone.

"I've missed you a whole lot."

"Then how come you didn't call?"

"I've been in meetings day and night, Amanda. Besides, I figured if I heard your voice, I wouldn't be able to stop myself from walking into your office and taking you on your desk."

Amanda's cheeks burned, but she knew her eyes were sparkling. "Jordan," she protested in a whisper, "this is a public place."

"That's why you're not lying on the table with your skirt up around your waist," Jordan answered with a perfectly straight face.

"You have to be the most arrogant man I've ever met," Amanda told him, but a smile hovered around her mouth. She couldn't very well deny that Jordan could make her do extraordinary things.

The waiter returned with their seafood salads, sparing Jordan from having to answer. His reply probably would have been cocky, anyway, Amanda figured.

The conversation had turned to more conventional subjects, when Madge Brockman suddenly appeared beside the table. There was a look of infinite strain in her face as she assessed Amanda, then Jordan.

Amanda braced herself, having no idea whether to expect a civil greeting or violent recriminations. "Hello, Mrs. Brockman," she said as Jordan pushed back his chair to stand. "I'd like you to meet Jordan Richards."

"Do sit down," Madge Brockman said when she and Jordan had shaken hands.

Jordan remained standing. "How is your husband?" he asked, knowing Amanda wouldn't dare ask.

"He's recovering," Madge replied with a sigh. "And he's adamant about wanting a divorce."

"I'm sorry," Amanda said softly.

The older woman managed a faulty smile. "I'll get over it, I guess. Well, if you'll excuse me, I'm supposed to meet my attorney, and I see him sitting right over there."

Jordan dropped back into his chair when Mrs. Brockman had walked away. "Are you okay?" he asked.

Amanda pushed her salad away. Even though she'd done it inadvertently, she was partly responsible for destroying Mrs. Brockman's marriage, and the knowledge was shattering. "No," she answered. "I'm not okay."

"It wasn't your fault, Amanda."

There it was again, that strange clairvoyance of his.

"Yes, it was—part of it, at least. I didn't even bother to ask if James was married. And now look what's happening."

Jordan gave a ragged sigh. Apparently his appetite had fled, too, for he set down his fork and sank back in his chair, one hand to his chin.

"The man's marital status wouldn't have made a difference to a lot of women, you know," he remarked. "For instance, you're the first one I've dated who's asked me whether I was married."

"Okay, so infidelity is widespread. So is cocaine addiction. That doesn't make either of them right."

Jordan raised his eyebrows. "I wasn't saying it did, Mandy. My point is, you're being too damn hard on yourself. So you made a mistake. Welcome to the human race."

Amanda met Jordan's gaze. "Were you faithful to Becky?" she asked, having no idea why it was suddenly so important to know. But it was.

"That's none of your damn business," Jordan retorted politely, making a steeple under his chin with his hands, "but I'll answer, anyway. I was true to my wife, and she was true to me."

Amanda had known, in some corner of her heart, that Jordan was a man of his word, and she believed him. "Were you ever tempted?"

"About a thousand times," he replied. "But there's a difference between thinking about something and doing it, Mandy. Now, do you want to ask me about my bank balance or my tax return? Or maybe how I voted in the last election?"

Amanda smiled. "You've made your point, Mr. Richards. I'm being nosy. But I'm glad you were faithful to Becky."

"So am I," Jordan said, as by tacit agreement they rose to go. "When am I going to see you again, Mandy?"

Amanda held off answering until the bill was paid and they were walking down the sidewalk, wending their way through hordes of Christmas shoppers. "When do you want to see me?"

"As soon as possible."

"You could come to dinner tonight."

"Amanda Scott, you have a silver tongue. I'll bring the wine and the food, so don't cook."

Amanda's smile was born deep inside her, and it took its time reaching her mouth. "Seven?"

"Eight," Jordan said as they stopped in front of the Evergreen Hotel. "I have a meeting, and it might run late."

She stood on tiptoe to kiss him briefly. "I'll be waiting, Mr. Richards."

He grinned as he rubbed a tendril of her hair between his fingers. "Good," he answered.

His voice made Amanda's knees quiver beneath her green suede skirt.

When Amanda reached her desk, there was a message waiting for her. In a flash, work—and Jordan—fled her uppermost thoughts. The hospital had called about James, and the matter was urgent.

Amanda's fingers trembled as she reached for the panel of buttons on her telephone. She punched out the numbers written on the message slip and, when an operator answered, asked for the designated extension.

"Intensive Care," a sunny voice said when the call was put through. "This is Betsy Andrews."

Amanda sank into her desk chair, a terrible headache throbbing beneath her temples. "My name is Amanda Scott," she said in a voice that sounded surprisingly crisp and professional. "I received a message asking me to call about Mr. Brockman."

There was a short silence while the nurse checked her records. "Yes. Mr. Brockman isn't doing very well, Ms. Scott. And he's constantly asking for you."

Amanda closed her eyes and rubbed one temple with her fingertips. She'd broken up with James long ago, and had refused his gifts and his requests for a reconciliation. When was it going to be over? "I see."

"His wife has explained the—er—situation to us," the nurse went on, "but Mr. Brockman still insists on seeing you."

"What is his doctor's recommendation?"

"It was his idea that we call you. We all feel that, well, maybe Mr. Brockman would calm down if he could just have a short visit from you."

Amanda glanced at her watch. Her headache was so intense that the numbers blurred. "I could stop by briefly after work." James had won this round. Under the circumstances, there was no way she could refuse to visit him. "That would be about six o'clock."

Betsy Andrews sounded relieved. "I'll be off duty then, but I'll make a note in the record and tell Mr. Brockman you'll be coming in."

"Thank you," Amanda said with a defeated sigh. Once she'd hung up, she reached for the phone again, planning to call Jordan, but her hand fell back to the desk. She was a grown woman, and this was her problem, not Jordan's. She couldn't go running to him every time some difficulty came up.

Pulling open her desk drawer, Amanda took out a bottle of aspirin, shook two tablets into her palm and swallowed them with water from the tap in her bathroom. Then she rolled up her sleeves and did her best to concentrate on her work.

At six-fifteen she approached James's door in the Intensive Care Unit, having gotten directions from a nurse.

He was lying in a room banked with flowers. Tubes led into his nose and the veins in both his hands. He seemed to sense Amanda's arrival and turned to look at her.

She approached the bed. "Hello, James," she said.

"You came," he managed, his voice hoarse and broken.

She nodded, unable for the moment to speak. And not knowing what to say.

"I'm going to die," he told her.

Amanda shook her head, her eyes filling with tears. She didn't love James anymore, but she had once, and it was hard to see him suffer. "No."

His eyes half-closed, he pleaded with her, "Just tell me there's a chance for us, and I'll have a reason not to give up."

Amanda started to tell him there was someone else, that there could never be anything between the two of them again, but something stopped her in the last instant. Some instinct that he really meant to die if she didn't give him hope, and she couldn't just abandon him to death. She bit down on her lower lip, then whispered, "All right, James. Maybe we could—start again."

# 8

Jordan was due to arrive a little more than twenty minutes after Amanda reached her apartment. Gershwin was hungry and petulant, and the boxes containing the fur jacket and the skimpy bikini James had sent were still sitting on the hallway table. Amanda had intended to return them to the department store and ask the clerk to credit James's account, but she hadn't gotten around to it.

Now, without stopping to analyze her motives—certainly she meant to tell Jordan about her promise to James—she stuffed the boxes into the back of her bedroom closet and hastily changed into a silky beige jumpsuit. She had just misted herself with cologne, when the door buzzer sounded.

After drawing a deep breath to steady herself, Amanda dashed through the apartment and opened the door. Jordan was standing in the hallway, a tired grin on his face, a bottle of wine and several bags from a Chinese take-out place in his arms.

Looking at him, Amanda thought of how it would be to have him walk out of her life forever, and promptly lost her courage. She told herself it wasn't the right time to tell him about James.

Smiling shakily, she took the wine and fragrant bags from him and stood on tiptoe to kiss his cheek.

He shrugged out of his overcoat and hung it on the coat tree while Amanda carried the food to the table. She hadn't put out place settings yet, so she hurried back to the kitchenette for plates, silverware, wineglasses and a cork screw.

Jordan looked at her strangely when she returned. "Is something wrong, Mandy?"

Amanda swallowed. *Tell him,* ordered the voice of reason. *Just come right out and tell him you're planning to visit James in the hospital until he's out of danger.* "Wr-wrong?" she echoed.

"You seem nervous."

Amanda imagined the scenario: herself telling Jordan that she meant to pretend she was still in love with James just until he was stronger, Jordan saying the idea was stupid, getting angry, walking out. Maybe forever. "I'm okay," she lied.

Jordan popped the cork on the wine bottle. "If you say so," he said with a sigh, and they both sat down at the table to consume prawns, fried noodles and chow mein. Their conversation, usually so free and easy, was guarded.

When they were through with dinner, Jordan made Amanda stay at the table, nursing a second glass of wine, while he cleared away the debris of their meal. Returning, he put gentle hands on Amanda's shoulders and began massaging her tense muscles.

"Will you stay tonight?" she asked, holding her breath after the words were out. She needed Jordan desperately, but at the same time she knew guilt would prevent her from enjoying their lovemaking.

Jordan sighed. "You've been through a lot lately, Mandy. I think it would be better if we let things cool off a little."

She turned to look up at him with worried eyes. "Is this the brush-off, Mr. Richards?"

He smiled and bent to kiss her forehead. "No. I just think you need some extra rest." With that, he turned and crossed the room to the entryway. He reached for his overcoat and put it on.

Amanda stood up quickly and went to him. Even though Jordan didn't know what was going on, he sensed something, and he was already distancing himself from her. She had to tell him. "Jordan—"

He interrupted her with a kiss. "Good night, Mandy. I'll talk to you tomorrow."

Amanda tried to call out to him, but the words stopped in her throat. In the end she simply closed the door, locked it and stood there leaning against the panel, wondering how she'd gotten herself into such a mess.

True to his word, Jordan called her the next morning at work, but their conversation was brief because he was busy and so was Amanda. She threw her mind into her job in order to distract herself from the fact that she had, in effect, lied to him. And a chilling instinct told her that deceit was one thing Jordan wouldn't tolerate.

At six-thirty that evening, Amanda walked into James's room in Intensive Care, after first making sure Madge wasn't there. She was wearing jeans and a sweater, and was carrying a bouquet of flowers from the gift shop downstairs.

He smiled thinly when he saw her and extended one hand. "Hello, Amanda."

She took his hand and bent to kiss his forehead. "Hi. How are you feeling today?"

"They're moving me out of the ICU tomorrow," he answered.

But he looked very sick to Amanda. He was gaunt, and his skin still had a ghastly pallor to it.

"That's good."

"You look wonderful."

Amanda averted her eyes for a moment, feeling like a highly paid call girl. What she was doing was all wrong, but how could she turn her back on another human being, allowing him to give up and die? That would be heartless. "Thanks."

James's grip on her hand was remarkably firm. "You're better off without that Richards character," he confided. "He might have made his mark in the business world, but he's really nothing more than an overgrown kid. Killed his own wife with his recklessness, you know."

Amanda was willing to go only so far with this charade, and listening to James bad-mouth Jordan was beyond the boundary. Somewhat abruptly she changed the subject. "Is there anything you'd like me to bring you? Magazines or books?"

He shook his head. "All I want is to know I'm going to get well and see you wear—and not wear—that blue bikini."

Feeling slightly ill, Amanda nonetheless managed a smile. "You shouldn't be thinking thoughts like that," she scolded. She had to get out of that room or soon she'd be smothered. "Listen, the nurses made me promise not to stay too long, so I'm going now. But I'll be back after work tomorrow."

When she would have walked away, James held her fast by the hand. "I want a kiss first," he said, a shrewd expression in his eyes.

Amanda shook her head, unable to grant his request. She smiled brittlely and said in a too-bright voice, "You're too ill for that." Ignoring his obvious disappointment, she squeezed his hand once and then dashed out of the room, calling a hasty farewell over her shoulder.

Only when Amanda was outside in the crisp December air was she able to breathe properly again. She went home, flung her coat onto the couch and took a long, scalding hot shower. No matter how she tried, though, she couldn't wash away the awful feeling that she was selling herself.

In an effort to escape, Amanda telephoned the real estate agency on Vashon Island the next morning to see if the Victorian house had been sold. It hadn't, and even though she had no means of buying it herself, the news lifted her flagging spirits.

She visited James that night, and the next, and he seemed to be improving steadily. He told her repeatedly that she was his only reason for holding on.

By Friday, when Eunice was due to arrive, Amanda was practically a wreck. She had been avoiding Jordan's calls for several days, and she could barely concentrate on her job.

Marion noticed her elder daughter's general dishevelment when they met at the airport in front of the gate assigned to Eunice's flight. "What on earth is the matter with you?" she demanded. "You have bags under your eyes and you must have lost five pounds since I saw you last week!"

Amanda would have given anything to be able to confide in her mother, but she didn't want to spoil Eunice's homecoming—her sister would need all of Marion's and Bob's support. She shrugged and managed a halfhearted smile. "You know how it is. Falling in love takes a lot out of a person."

Marion's gaze was slightly narrowed and alarmingly shrewd. "You're not fooling me, you know," she said. "But just because I don't have time to drag it out of you now doesn't mean I won't."

Bob was just returning from parking the car, and he smiled and gave Amanda a hug. "You're looking a little peaky," he pointed out good-naturedly.

"She's up to something," Marion informed him just before the passengers from Eunice's flight began pouring out of the gate.

Amanda was the first to reach her brown-eyed, dark-haired sister, and they embraced. Tears stung both their eyes.

After the usual hassles of getting the luggage from the baggage carousel and fighting the traffic out of the airport, they drove back to the family home. Eunice chattered the whole time about how glad she was to be in Seattle again, how miserable she'd been in California, how she wished she'd never met Jim, let alone married him. By the time they reached the quiet residential area where Bob and Marion lived, Eunice had exhausted herself.

She stumbled into the room she and Amanda had once shared and collapsed on one of the twin beds.

Amanda took a seat on the other one. "I'm glad you're back," she said.

Her sister sat up on the bed and began unbuttoning her coat. "I didn't exactly return in triumph, like I thought I would," Eunice observed sadly. "Oh, Amanda, my life is a disaster area."

"I know what you mean," Amanda answered sadly, thinking of the deception she hadn't had the courage to straighten out.

Eunice yawned. "Maybe tomorrow we can put our heads together and figure out how to get ourselves back on track."

With a smile, Amanda opened her sister's suitcase and found a nightgown for her. "Here," she said, tossing the billow of pink chiffon into Eunice's lap. "Get some sleep."

When Eunice had disappeared into the adjoining bathroom, Amanda returned to the kitchen. Her mother was sitting at the table, sipping decaffeinated coffee, and Bob was in the living room, listening to the news.

"How's Eunice?" Marion asked.

Amanda wedged her hands into the front pockets of her worn brown corduroy pants. "She'll be okay once she gets a perspective on things."

"And what about you?"

"I'm in a fix, Mom," Amanda admitted, staring at the darkened window over the kitchen sink. "And I don't know how to get out of it."

Marion went to the counter, poured a cup of coffee from the percolator and brought it back to the table for Amanda. "Sit down and tell me about it."

Amanda sank into the chair. "Some very good things have been happening between Jordan and me," she said, closing her fingers around the cup to warm them. "I never thought I'd meet anybody like him."

Marion smiled. "I feel the same way about Bob."

Amanda touched her mother's hand fondly. "I know."

"So what's the problem?"

"About a week ago," Amanda began reluctantly, "someone from the hospital called and said James was asking for me. He was in the ICU at the time, so I didn't feel I could ignore the whole thing. I went to see him, and while I was there, he told me he'd given up, that he was going to die."

Marion's lips thinned in irritation, but she seemed to know how hard it was for Amanda to keep up her momentum, so she didn't interrupt.

"Essentially, he said I was the only reason he had to go on living, and if I didn't want him, he was just going to give up. So I've been visiting him and pretending we'll be getting back together again once he's well."

Marion sighed heavily. "Amanda."

"I know it sounds crazy, but I feel guilty enough without being the reason somebody died!"

Marion reached out and covered Amanda's hand with her own. "I suppose you haven't told Jordan any of this."

"I'm afraid to. Maybe it would have been all right if I'd mentioned it that very first night after I spoke to James, when Jordan and I were together for dinner, but I couldn't bring myself to do it. I was too afraid he'd make me choose between him and James."

"I didn't think there was any question of a choice," Marion said. "You're in love with Jordan Richards, whether you know it or not."

Amanda bit her lower lip for a moment. "I guess I am."

"Tell him the truth, Amanda," Marion urged. "Don't put it off for another second. March right over to that phone and call him."

"I can't," Amanda said with a shake of her head. "It's not something I can say over the telephone, and besides, his little girls will be there. This is their first night together, and I don't want to spoil it."

"You're going to regret it if you don't straighten this out," Marion warned.

"I think it might already be too late," Amanda said brokenly, and then she rose from her chair, emptied her coffee into the sink and set the cup down. "You just concentrate on Eunice, Mom, and don't worry about me."

Marion shook her head as she got up to see her daughter to the door. "Talk to Jordan," she insisted as Amanda put on her coat and wrapped a colorful knitted scarf around her neck.

Amanda nodded and hurried through the cold night to her car.

The light on her answering machine was blinking when she arrived home, and after brewing herself a cup of tea, she pushed the Play button and sat down at the little table in her living room to listen.

The first call was from James. He'd missed her that night and hoped she'd come to visit in the morning.

Amanda closed her eyes against the prospect, though she knew she would have to do as he asked. Maybe if she used Eunice's visit as an excuse, she could get away after only a half hour or so.

The next message nearly made her spill her tea. "This is Madge Brockman," an angry female voice said, "and I just wanted to tell you that you're not going to get away with this. You took my husband, and I'm going to take something from you." After those bitter words, the woman had hung up with a crash.

Amanda was struggling to compose herself, when yet another voice came on. "Mandy, this is Jordan. I've survived supper, and the kids' baths and story time. I have a new respect for mothers. Call me, will you?" There was a click, and then the machine rewound itself.

Despite the fact that Madge Brockman's call had shaken her to her soul, Amanda reached for the phone and dialed Jordan's number at the island house.

He answered on the second ring.

"Hi, Jordan. It's Amanda."

"Thank God," he replied with a lilt to his voice.

"How are the girls?" She dabbed at her eyes with her sleeve and resisted an impulse to sniffle.

"They're fine. Mandy, are you all right?"

"I—I need to see you. Could I c-come out there?"

Jordan hesitated, then said, "Sure. If you hurry, you can still make the last ferry. Mandy—"

"I'll be there as soon as I can," Amanda broke in, and then she hung up the phone and dashed into her bedroom. She pulled her suitcase out from under the bed and tossed in two pairs of jeans, two sets of clean underwear and two sweaters. Then, after snatching up her toothbrush and makeup bag, she made sure Gershwin had plenty of food and water and hurried out of the apartment.

Several times on the way to West Seattle Amanda's eyes were so full of tears that she nearly had to pull over to the side of the road. But finally she drove on board the ferry and parked.

Safe in the bottom of the enormous boat, she let her forehead rest against the steering wheel and sobbed.

By the time she'd reached Vashon Island and driven to Jordan's house, however, she was beginning to feel a little foolish. She wasn't a child, she told herself sternly, and she couldn't expect Jordan to solve her problems. She might have backed out of the driveway and raced back to the ferry dock if Jordan hadn't come outside to greet her.

He was wearing sneakers, jeans and a Seahawks sweatshirt, and he looked so good to Amanda that she nearly burst into tears again.

Without a word, he opened the door and helped her out, then fetched her suitcase and overnighter from the back seat. Amanda preceded him into the house, wondering what she was going to say.

There was a fire snapping on the hearth, and after setting her luggage down in the entryway, Jordan helped Amanda out of her coat. "Sit down and I'll get you some brandy," he said hoarsely after kissing her on the cheek.

Amanda took a seat on the raised stone hearth of the fireplace, hoping the warmth would take the numb chill out of her soul.

When Jordan sat down next to her and handed her a crystal snifter with brandy glowing golden in the bottom, her heart turned over. She knew she'd waited too long to explain things; she was going to lose him.

"Talk to me, Mandy," he said when she was silent, studying him with miserable eyes.

"I can't," she replied, setting the brandy aside untouched. "Will you just hold me, Jordan? Just for a few minutes?"

Gently he pulled her into his arms and pressed her head to his shoulder. He moved his hand soothingly up and down her back, but he didn't ask any questions or make any demands, and Amanda loved him more than ever for that.

Amanda had just about worked up her courage to tell him about her promise to James, when a small, curious voice asked, "Who's that, Daddy?"

Amanda started in Jordan's arms, but he held her fast. She turned her head and saw a little dark-haired girl standing a few feet away. She was wearing a pink quilted robe and tiny fluffy slippers to match.

"This is Amanda, Jess. Amanda, my daughter, Jessica."

"Hi," Amanda managed.

"How come you're hugging her?" Jessica wanted to know. "Did she fall down and hurt herself?"

"Sort of," Jordan answered. "Why don't you go back to bed now, honey? You can get to know Amanda better in the morning."

Jessica's smile was so like Becky's that Amanda was shaken by it. "Okay. Good night, Daddy. Good night, Amanda."

When the little girl was gone, Amanda sat there in Jordan's arms, sorely wishing she hadn't intruded. She didn't belong here.

"I shouldn't have come," she said, bolting to her feet.

Jordan pulled her back so that she landed on his lap. "You've missed the last ferry, Mandy," he pointed out. "Besides, I'm not letting you go anywhere in the shape you're in."

Amanda swallowed hard. "I can't sleep with you—not with your daughters in the house."

"I understand that," Jordan replied. "I have a guest room."

Why did he have to be so damned reasonable? Amanda fretted. She didn't deserve his patience or his kindness. "Okay," she said lamely, reaching for her brandy and downing the whole thing practically in one gulp. Maybe that would give her the courage to say what she needed to say.

But it only made her woozy and very nauseous. Jordan lifted her into his arms and carried her to the guest room, where he undressed her like a weary child, put her into one of his pajama tops because she'd forgotten to bring a nightgown and tucked her in.

"Jordan, I made a terrible mistake."

He kissed her forehead. "We'll talk tomorrow," he said. "Go to sleep."

Exhaustion immediately conquered Amanda, and when she awakened, it was morning. Jordan had brought her things to her room. There was a small bathroom adjoining, so she showered, brushed her teeth and put on make-up. When she arrived in the kitchen, wearing jeans and a blue sweater, she felt a hundred percent better than she had the night before.

Jordan was making pancakes on an electric griddle and cooking bacon in the microwave, while his daughters sat at the table, drinking their orange juice and watching him with amusing consternation. While Jessica resembled Becky, the smaller child, Lisa, looked like Jordan. She had his maple-brown hair and hazel eyes, and she smiled broadly when she saw Amanda.

Again, despite her improved mood, Amanda felt like an imposter shoving herself in where she didn't belong. She would have fled to her car if she hadn't known it would only compound her problems.

"Hungry?" Jordan asked, his eyes gentle as he studied Amanda's face.

She nodded, and, seeing that there were four places set at the table, took a chair beside Lisa.

"That's Daddy's chair," Jessica pointed out.

Amanda started to move, but Jordan slapped his hand down on her shoulder and pushed her back.

"It doesn't matter where Amanda sits," he said.

Jessica didn't take offense at the correction, and Amanda reached for the orange juice carton with a trembling hand. She was more than ready to tell

Jordan the truth now, but it didn't look as though she was going to get the opportunity. After all, she couldn't just drop an emotional bombshell in front of his daughters.

Jordan's cooking was good, and Amanda managed to put away three pancakes and a couple of strips of bacon even though she couldn't remember the last time she'd been so nervous.

"I think it's about time we decorated that Christmas tree, don't you?" Jordan asked when the meal was over.

The girls gave a rousing cheer and bounded out of their chairs and into the living room.

"You'll have to get dressed first," Jordan called after them. Despite his lack of experience, he seemed to be picking up the fundamentals of active fatherhood rather easily.

"Lisa can't tie her shoes," Jessica confided from the kitchen doorway.

"Then you can do it for her," Jordan replied, beginning to clear the table.

Amanda insisted on helping, and the moment Jordan heard the kids' feet pounding up the stairway, he took her into his arms and gave her a thorough kiss. She melted against him, overpowered, as always, by his strange magic.

"It's very good to have you here, lady," he said in a rumbling whisper. "I just wish I could take you upstairs and spend about two hours making love to you."

Amanda shivered at the prospect. She wished that, too, with all her heart, but once she told Jordan about her visits to James's hospital room and her pretense of rekindling their affair, he probably wouldn't ever want to touch her again.

The idea of never lying in Jordan's arms another night, never feeling the weight of his body or going crazy under the touch of his hands or his mouth, made a hard lump form in her throat.

"Still not ready to talk?" he asked, touching the tip of her nose with a gentle finger.

Amanda shook her head.

"There's time," Jordan said, and he kissed her again, making her throw her arms around his neck in an instinctive plea for more.

"Daddy!" a little voice shouted from upstairs. "I can't find my red shoes!"

Amanda pushed away from Jordan as though he'd struck her, and lifted the back of one hand to her mouth when he turned away to go and help his daughter.

While he was gone, Amanda's bravery completely deserted her. She found her purse and dashed for her car, leaving her luggage behind in Jordan's guest room. He ran outside just as she pulled out of the driveway, but Amanda didn't stop. She put her foot down hard on the accelerator and drove away.

A glance at her watch told her the ferry wouldn't leave for another twenty minutes, and Amanda was half-afraid Jordan would toss the kids in the car and come chasing after her. Since she couldn't face him, she drove to the café where they'd eaten on a couple of occasions.

After parking her car behind a delivery truck, Amanda went into the restaurant, took a chair as far from the front door as she could and hid behind her menu until Wanda arrived.

"Well, hello there," the pleasant woman boomed. "Where's Jordan?"

"He's—busy. Could I get a cup of coffee?"

Wanda arched one artfully plucked eyebrow, but she didn't ask any more questions. She just brought a cup to Amanda's table and filled it from the pot in her other hand.

"Thanks," Amanda said, wishing she didn't have to give up the menu.

Jordan didn't show up, and Amanda was half disappointed and half relieved. She finished her coffee and went back to the ferry terminal just in time to board the boat.

Because she hoped there would be a message on the answering machine from Jordan and feared there would not, she went to the hospital first, instead of her apartment.

"You're late," James fussed when she walked into his room.

"I'm sorry—" Amanda began.

She'd forgotten what a master James was of the quicksilver change, and the brightness of his smile stunned her. "That's okay," he said generously. "I'm just glad you're here."

Amanda lowered her eyes. She would have given anything to be with Jordan and his children at that moment, helping to decorate the Christmas tree or even listening to a lecture. She regretted giving in to her impulse and running away. "Me, too," she lied.

"Tell me you love me," James said.

Amanda's heart stopped beating. She would have choked on the words if she'd tried to utter them.

For better or worse, Madge Brockman spared her the trouble. "Isn't this sweet?" she asked, sweeping like a storm into the room in a black full-length mink with a matching hat. Her eyes, full of poison, swung to Amanda. "To think I believed you when you said you and James were through."

"Amanda and I are going to be married," James protested, and he raised one hand to his chest.

Amanda was terrified.

"You idiot," Madge growled at him, gesturing wildly with one mink-swathed arm. "She's two-timing you with Jordan Richards!"

"That's a lie!" James shouted.

A nurse burst into the room. "Mr. Brockman, you must be calm!"

Terrified, Amanda backed blindly out into the hallway and ran to the elevator. It seemed to be her day for running away, she thought to herself as she got into her car and sped out of the parking lot.

For a time she just drove around Seattle, following an aimless path, trying to gather her composure. She considered visiting her mother, or one of her friends, but she couldn't, because she knew she'd break down and cry if she tried to explain things to anyone.

Finally Amanda drove back to her apartment building and went in through the rear entrance.

In the bathroom she splashed cold water on her face, washing away the tearstains, but her eyes were still puffy afterward, and her nose was an unglamorous red. It was no real surprise when the door buzzer sounded.

"Jordan or the tiger?" she asked herself with a sort of wounded fancy as she made her way determinedly across the living room and reached for the doorknob.

# 9

Jordan stood in the hallway, holding Amanda's suitcase. He was alone, and his expression was quietly contemptuous.

For the moment Amanda couldn't speak, so she stepped back to let him pass. He set the luggage down with a clatter just inside the entryway and jammed his hands into the pockets of his leather jacket.

"Why the hell did you run off like that?" he demanded.

For a second or so, Amanda swung wildly between relief and dread. She turned away from Jordan, walked to the sofa and sank onto it. "You haven't had a call from Mrs. Brockman?" she asked in a small voice.

Without bothering to take off his jacket—he obviously didn't intend to stay long—Jordan perched on the arm of an easy chair. "James's wife? Why would she call me?"

Amanda swallowed. "I've been visiting James in the hospital," she blurted out. "I told him we could t-take up where we left off."

The color drained from Jordan's face. "What?"

"He said he was going to give up and die—that I was all he had to live for. So I decided to pretend I still loved him, just until he was strong enough to go on his own."

"And you believed that?" His voice was low, lethal.

"Of course I believed it!" Amanda flared.

"Well, you've been had," Jordan replied coldly.

Amanda stared at him, wounded, her worst suspicions confirmed. "I knew you wouldn't understand, Jordan," she said. "That's why I was afraid to tell you."

"Damn it," he rasped, "don't make excuses. A lie is a lie, Amanda, and there's no room in my life for games like this!"

"It wasn't a game! You didn't see him, hear him..."

Jordan was on his feet again, his hands back in his pockets. "I didn't have to." He walked to the door and stood there for a moment with his back to Amanda. "I could understand your wanting to help," he said in parting. "But I'll never understand why you didn't tell me about it." With that, he opened the door and walked out.

Amanda jumped off the couch and raced to the entryway—she couldn't lose him, she *couldn't*— but at the door she stopped. Jordan had judged her and found her guilty, and he wasn't going to change his mind.

It was over.

Slowly Amanda closed the door. With a concerned meow, Gershwin circled her ankles. "He's gone," she said to the cat, and then she went into the bedroom, found the fur jacket and the skimpy bikini, and returned to her car.

With every mile she drove, Amanda became more certain that Jordan had been right: James had used emotional blackmail to get her to come back to him. She could see now that he'd given a performance every time she'd visited his room; she recalled the shrewd expression in his eyes, the things he'd said about Jordan.

"Fool!" Amanda muttered to herself, flipping on her windshield wipers as a light rain began to fall.

When she reached the hospital, Amanda marched inside, carrying the fur coat over her arm and the bikini in her purse. Some of her resolution faded as she got into the elevator, though. James had a serious heart condition, and for a time he'd been in real danger. Suppose what she meant to say caused him to suffer another attack? Suppose he died and it was her fault?

Amanda approached James's room reluctantly, then stopped when she heard him laughing. "Face it, Richards," he said. "You lose. In
another week or two I'll be out of this place. And
believe me, Amanda will be more than happy to
fly off to Hawaii with me and make sure I recuperate properly."

Her first instinct was to flee, but Amanda
couldn't move. She stood frozen in the hallway,
resting one hand against the wall.

Jordan said something in response, but
Amanda didn't hear what it was—maybe because
the thundering of her heart drowned it out.

The scraping of a chair broke Amanda's spell,
and she didn't know whether to stay and face Jordan or dodge into the little nook across the hall
where a coffee machine stood. In the end she decided she'd done enough running away for a lifetime, and stayed where she was.

When Jordan walked out of James's room, he
stopped cold for a moment, but then a weary expression of resignation came over his face.

"I'm going to tell him the truth," she said, her
voice hardly more than a whisper.

Jordan shrugged. "It's a little late for that, isn't
it?" His eyes dropped to the rich sable jacket
draped over her arm. "Merry Christmas, Amanda."

Amanda saw all her hopes going down the drain, and something inside drove her to fight to save them. "Jordan, be reasonable. You know I never meant for things to turn out this way!"

He looked at her for a moment, then walked around her, as he would something objectionable lying on the sidewalk, and strode off down the hall.

Amanda watched him go into the elevator. He looked straight through her as the doors closed.

It was a few moments before she could bring herself to walk into James's room and face him. She no longer feared that her news would cause him another heart attack; now it was her anger she struggled to control.

Finally she was able to force herself through the doorway. She laid the coat at the foot of James's bed without meeting his eyes, then took the bikini from her purse and put it with the coat. When she thought she could manage it without hysterics, she turned to him and said, "You had no right to manipulate me that way."

"Amanda." His voice was a scolding drawl, and he stretched out his hand to her.

She evaded his grasp. "It's over, James. I can't see you anymore."

Surprisingly James smiled at her and let his hand fall to his side. "You might as well come back to me, baby. It's plain enough that Richards is through with you."

Hot rage made Amanda's backbone ramrod straight, but she didn't allow her anger to erupt in a flow of nasty retorts. Clinging to the last of her dignity, she whispered, "Maybe the time I had with Jordan will have to last me a lifetime. But he's the only man I'll ever love." With that, she turned and walked out.

"You'll be back!" James shouted after her. "You'll come begging for my forgiveness! Damn it, Amanda, nobody walks out on me...."

While a nurse rushed into James's room, Amanda went straight on until she got to the elevator. She pushed the button and waited circumspectly for a ride to the main floor, even though her emotions were howling in her spirit like a storm. She wanted to be anywhere but there, anybody besides herself.

She'd hoped Jordan might be lingering somewhere downstairs, or maybe in her section of the parking lot, but there was no sign of him.

Beyond tears, she climbed behind the wheel of her car and started toward the house where she and Eunice had grown up.

She knocked at the door and called out "It's me!" and her mother instantly replied with a cheerful "Come in!"

Bob, it turned out, was putting in some overtime at the aircraft plant where he worked, but Marion and Eunice were wrapping festive presents on the dining room table. Eunice looked a little tired, but other than that she seemed to be in good spirits. Marion was taking her usual delight in the yuletide season, but her face fell when she got a look at her elder daughter.

"Merciful heavens," she sputtered, rushing over and forcing Amanda into a chair. "You're as pale as Marley's ghost! What on earth is the matter?"

Just minutes before, Amanda had been convinced she had no tears left to cry, but now a despondent wail escaped her and tears streamed down her face.

Eunice immediately rushed to her side. "Sis, what is it?" she whispered, near tears herself. She had always cried whenever Amanda did, even if she didn't know what was bothering her sister.

"It's Jordan!" Amanda sobbed. "He's gone— he never wants to see me again. . . ."

"Get her a glass of water," Marion said to Eunice. She rested her hands on Amanda's shoulders, much as Jordan once had, trying to soothe away the terrible tension.

Eunice reappeared moments later, looking stricken, a glass of water in one hand.

"You told him," Marion said as Amanda sipped the cold water.

Eunice dragged up a chair beside her. "Told him what?"

Setting the water down with a thump, Amanda blurted out the whole story—how she'd fallen hopelessly in love with Jordan, how James had hoodwinked her into ruining everything. She ended with an account of the scene in James's hospital room when she'd given back his gifts once and for all.

"What kind of lunkhead is this Jordan," Eunice demanded, "that he doesn't understand something so simple?"

Amanda dragged her sleeve across her eyes, feeling like a five-year-old with both knees skinned raw. Only it was her heart that was hurting. "He's angry because I didn't tell him about it from the first." She paused to sniffle, and her mother produced a handful of tissues in that magical way mothers have. "I tried, I honestly did, but I was so scared of losing him."

"Men," muttered Eunice. "Who needs them?"

"I do," chorused Amanda and Marion. And at that, all three women laughed.

Eunice patted Amanda's shoulder. "Don't worry. After he thinks about it for a while, he'll forgive you."

Amanda shook her head, dabbing at her puffy eyes with a wad of damp tissue. "You don't know

Jordan. He's probably never told a lie in his life. He just flat out doesn't understand deception.''

''Maybe he's never lied,'' Marion said briskly, ''but he's made mistakes, just like the rest of us. When he calms down, Amanda, he'll call.''

Amanda prayed her mother was right, but the hollow feeling in the center of her heart made that seem unlikely.

An hour later, when Amanda announced that she was going home, Eunice grabbed her coat and insisted on riding along. She'd make supper, she said, and the two of them could just hang around the way they had in high school.

''I wasn't planning to stick my head in the oven or anything, if that's what you're worried about,'' Amanda said with a sad smile as she backed her car out of her parents' driveway.

Eunice grinned. ''And singe those gorgeous, golden tresses? I should hope not.''

Amanda laughed at the image. ''You know what, kid? It's good to have you back.''

Her younger sister patted her arm. ''I'll be around awhile, I think,'' she replied. ''There's an opening for a computer programmer at the university. I have an interview the day after Christmas.''

''There's really no hope of getting back together with Jim, then?'' Amanda asked as they wended their way through rainy streets, the windshield wipers beating out a rhythmic accompaniment to their conversation.

Eunice shook her head. "Not when there's somebody else involved," she said.

Amanda nodded. Just the idea of Jordan seeing another woman was more than she could tolerate, even with the relationship in ruins.

After parking the car, Amanda and Eunice dashed through the rain to the store on the corner and bought popcorn, a log for the fireplace, a pound of fresh shrimp and the makings for a salad.

Back at Amanda's apartment, Eunice prepared and cooked the succulent shrimp while Amanda washed and cut up the vegetables.

"You don't even have a Christmas tree," Eunice complained later when she was kneeling on the hearth, lighting the paper-wrapped log.

Amanda shrugged. "I was just planning to skip the whole holiday," she said.

"Knowing Jordan didn't change that?"

"When I was with him, he was all I thought about," Amanda explained. "Same thing when I wasn't with him."

Eunice grinned and got to her feet, dusting her hands off on the legs of her jeans as if she'd just carried wood in from the wilderness like a pioneer. "You could always throw yourself at his feet and beg for forgiveness."

Amanda lifted her chin stubbornly and went to the living room window. "I explained everything to him, and he wouldn't listen."

Rain pattered at the glass and made the people on the sidewalks below hurry along under their colorful umbrellas. Amanda wondered how many of them were happy and how many had broken hearts.

"You shouldn't give up if you really care about the guy," Eunice said softly.

Amanda sighed. "I didn't give up, Eunice," she said. "He did."

At that, the two sisters dropped the subject of Jordan and talked about other Christmases.

Jordan had his own reasons for welcoming the rain, and after he drove on board the ferry to Vashon Island, he stayed in the car, staring bleakly at the empty van ahead of him. He felt hollow and numb, as though all his vitals had shriveled up and disappeared, but he knew the pain would come eventually, and he dreaded it.

After losing Becky, Jordan had made up his mind never to really care about another woman again. That way, he'd reasoned in his naïveté, he'd never have to suffer the way he had after his wife's death.

The trouble was, he'd reckoned without Amanda Scott.

He'd fallen hard for her without ever really being aware of what was happening. Had he told her that he loved her? He couldn't remember.

Maybe things would have been different if he had.

Jordan shook his head. He was being stupid. Telling her he cared wouldn't have prevented her from deceiving him. He drifted into a restless sleep, haunted by dreams of things that might have been, and when the ferry's horn blasted, he was startled. He hadn't been aware of the passing time.

Once the boat docked and his turn came, Jordan drove down the ramp, just as he had a million times before. Rain danced on the pavement, and wet gulls hid out beneath the picnic tables in the park he passed. The world was the same, and yet it was different.

He was alone again.

When he entered the kitchen through the garage door minutes later, he heard the stereo blasting. Taking off his jacket and running a hand through his rumpled hair, he went into the living room.

Jessie and Lisa had dragged their presents out from under the mammoth Christmas tree he and Amanda had chosen together, and piled them up in two teetering stacks. The baby-sitter, a teenage girl from down the road, was curled up on the couch, chattering into the telephone receiver.

Sighting Jordan, his daughters flung themselves at him with shrieks of glee, and he lifted one in each arm, making the growling sound they loved and pretending to be bent on chewing off their ears.

The baby-sitter, a plain little thing with thick glasses, hung up the telephone and tiptoed over to the stereo to turn it off.

Jordan let the girls down to the floor, took out his wallet and paid the sitter. The moment she was gone, Jessie folded her arms and announced, "Lisa has more presents than I do."

Jordan pretended to be horrified. "No!"

"Count them for yourself," Jessie challenged.

He knelt and began to count. The red-and-silver striped package on the top of Lisa's stack turned out to be the culprit. "This one is for both of you," Jordan said, tapping at the gift tag with his finger. "See? It's says 'Lisa *and* Jessie.' "

Jessie examined the tag studiously and was then satisfied that it was still a just world. "Where did Amanda go?" she asked, looking at him with Becky's eyes. "Why did she run away?"

Jordan had no idea how to explain Amanda's abrupt disappearance. He still didn't understand it completely himself. "She's at her apartment, I guess," he finally answered.

"But why did she runned away?" Lisa asked, rubbing her eye with the back of one dimpled hand.

"She probably went to heaven, like Mommy," Jessie said importantly.

Her innocent words went through Jordan like a lance. Young as they were, these kids were developing a strategy for being left—Mommy went to heaven; Daddy doesn't have time for us; Amanda was just passing through.

Jordan kissed both his girls resoundingly on the forehead. "Amanda's not in heaven," he said, sounding hoarse even to himself. "She's in Seattle. Now put these presents back under the tree before Santa finds out you've been messing around with them and fills your stockings with clam shells."

The telephone rang just as Jordan was rising to his feet, but he didn't lunge for it, even though that was his first instinct. He answered in a leisurely, offhand way, but his heart was pounding.

"Hi, little brother. It's Karen," his sister said warmly. "How are the monkeys getting along?"

Jordan forced himself to chuckle; he felt like weeping with disappointment. So it wasn't Amanda. What would he have said to her if it had been? "Do they always pile their presents in the middle of the living room?" he countered, trying to sound lighthearted.

Karen laughed. "No, that's a new one," she said. "How are you doing, Jord?"

He ran a hand through his hair. "Me? I'm doing great." *For somebody who's just had his insides torn out, that is.*

"No problems with memories?"

Jordan sighed and watched his children as they put their colorful gifts back underneath the tree. It seemed hard to believe there had ever been a time when he found it difficult even to look at them because they reminded him so much of Becky. "I guess I'm over that," he said huskily.

"Sounds to me like things are a little rocky."

Karen had always been perceptive. "It's something else," he said. The pain he'd been expecting was just starting to set in. "Listen, Karen, you and Paul and I have to have a talk about the girls. I want to spend more time with them."

"Took you long enough," Karen responded, her voice gentle.

Jordan remembered how she'd helped him through those dark days after Becky had died; she'd been there for him while he was in the hospital, and later, too. If she'd been in his living room instead of miles away on the peninsula, he'd have told her about Amanda.

"Better late than never," he finally replied.

"Paul and I will be down on Christmas Eve, as planned," Karen went on, probably sensing that

Jordan wasn't going to confide anything important over the phone. "Save some room under that tree, because we're bringing a carload of loot, and Becky's parents will send boxes of stuff."

Jordan chuckled and shook his head. "Just what they need," he said, watching the greedy munchkins playing tug-of-war with a box wrapped in shiny blue paper. "See you Christmas Eve, sis."

Karen said a few more words, then hung up.

"I'm hungry," said Lisa as a stain spread slowly through the fabric of her plaid jeans.

"She peed her pants," Jessie pointed out quite unnecessarily.

With a grin, Jordan swept his younger daughter up in his arms and carried her off to the bathroom.

'Twas the night before Christmas, and Amanda Scott was feeling sorry for herself. She sat with her feet up in front of the fire while her mother, stepfather and sister bundled up to go to the midnight service at church.

"No fair peeking in the stockings while we're gone," said Bob with a smile and a shake of his finger.

Marion and Eunice were less understanding. They both looked as though they wanted to shake her.

"Moping around this house won't change anything," Marion scolded.

"Yeah," Eunice agreed, gesturing. "Put on your coat and come with us."

"I'm wearing jeans and a sweatshirt, in case you haven't noticed," Amanda pointed out archly. Bob had on his best suit, and Marion and Eunice were both in new dresses.

"Nobody's going to notice," Marion fussed, and she looked so hopeful that Amanda would change her mind that Amanda relented and pushed herself out of the chair.

Soon, she was settled beside Eunice in the back seat of her parents' car. It was so much like the old days that for a while Amanda was able to pretend her life wasn't in ruins.

"Maybe a little angel will whisper in Jordan's ear and he'll call you," Eunice said in a low voice as Marion and Bob sang carols exuberantly in the front seat.

Amanda gave her sister a look. "And maybe Saint Nicholas will land on our roof tonight in a sleigh drawn by eight tiny reindeer."

"Okay, then," Eunice responded, bristling, "why don't you call him?"

The truth was that Amanda had dialed Jordan's number a hundred times since they'd parted. Once she'd even waited to hear him say hello before hanging up. "Gee, why don't I?" she retorted. "Or better yet, I could plunge headfirst off an overpass. I just *love* pain."

Eunice folded her arms. "Don't be such a poop, Amanda. I'm only trying to help."

"It isn't working," Amanda responded, turning her head to look out at the festive lights trimming roofs and windows and shrubbery.

The church service was soothing, as family traditions often are, and Amanda was feeling a little better when they drove back home. They all sat around the tree, sipping eggnog and listening to carols, and when Bob and Marion finally retired for the night, Eunice dug a package out from under a mountain of gifts and extended it.

Amanda accepted the present, but refused to open it until she had found her gift to Eunice. It was another tradition; as girls, the sisters had always made their exchange just before going to bed.

When Amanda opened her gift, she laughed. It was a copy of *Gathering Up the Pieces*, the same book she'd bought for Eunice.

Eunice was amazed when she opened her package. "I don't believe this," she whispered, a wide smile on her face. She turned back the flyleaf. "And it's autographed. Wow."

"I waited in line for hours to get it signed," Amanda exaggerated. She was remembering meeting Jordan that day, and feeling all the resultant pain.

"Let's go to bed and read ourselves to sleep," Eunice suggested, standing up and switching off the Christmas tree. Its veil of tinsel seemed to whisper a silvery song in the darkness.

"Good idea," Amanda answered.

She was all the way up to chapter three before she finally closed her eyes.

The kids were asleep and so, as far as Jordan knew, were Paul and Karen. He sat up in bed, switched on the lamp and reached for the telephone on the nightstand. The picture of Becky had been moved to a shelf in his study, but he looked at the place where it had stood and said, "Know what, Becky? I've got it bad."

A glance at his watch told him it was after two in the morning. If he called Amanda now, he would be sure to wake her up, but he didn't care. Whatever happened, he had to hear her voice and wish her a merry Christmas.

He punched out the number and waited, nervous as a high school kid. While the call went through, a number of scenarios came to mind— such as James answering with a sleepy "Hello." Or Amanda telling him to go straight to hell.

Instead he got a recorded voice. "Hi. This is Amanda Scott, and I can't come to the phone right now...."

Jordan hung up without leaving a message, switched off the light and lay back on his pillows. She was probably at her parents' place, he told himself.

Or maybe she was in Hawaii, helping James recuperate.

Jordan turned onto his stomach and slammed one fist into the pillow. He knew the lush plains and contours of Amanda's body, and he begrudged them to every other man on earth. They were his to touch, and no one else's.

His groin knotted as he recalled how it was to bury himself in Amanda's depths, to feel her hands moving on his back and the insides of her thighs against his hips. She'd lain beneath him like a temptress, her eyes smoldering, her body rising to meet his, stroke for stroke, her hands curled on the sides of the pillow.

But then, as release approached, she would bite down hard on her lower lip and roll her eyes back, focusing dreamily on nothing at all. A low, keening whimper would escape her as she surrendered completely, breaking past her clamped teeth to become a shameless groan...

Jordan sat bolt upright in bed and switched on the lamp again. He couldn't quite face the prospect of a cold shower, but he was too uncomfortable to stay where he was. He tossed back the covers, reached for his robe and tied it tightly around his waist. The cloth stood out like canvas stretched over a tent pole.

Feeling reasonably certain he wouldn't meet anybody, Jordan slipped out of his room and down the darkened stairs. In the kitchen he poured himself a glass of chocolate milk and carried it back to the living room. There he sat, staring at the silent glimmer of the dark Christmas tree, the bulging shapes of the stockings. The thin light of a winter moon poured in through the smoked-glass windows, making everything look unfamiliar.

"Jordan?" It was Karen's voice, and seconds before she switched on the lights, he grabbed a sofa pillow and laid it on his lap. His plump, pretty sister, bundled in her practical blue chenille robe, looked at him with concern. "Are you all right?"

"No," Jordan answered, tossing back the last of his chocolate milk as though it could give him the same solace as brandy or good whiskey. Since it was safe to set aside the pillow, he did. "Don't ever let anybody tell you it's 'better to have loved and lost, than never to have loved at all,'" he advised, sounding for all the world like a melancholy drunk. "I've done it twice, and I wish to God I'd joined the foreign legion, instead."

Karen sat down next to him. "So you're just going to give up, huh?"

"Yeah," Jordan answered obstinately. He had to change the subject, or risk being smothered in images of Amanda lying in somebody else's bed. "About the kids—"

"You want them back," Karen guessed with a gentle smile.

Jordan nodded.

_____ **10** _____

Amanda sat staring at the bank draft in amazement that dreary Saturday morning in February while a gray rain drizzled at the kitchen windows. "I don't understand," she muttered, glancing from Marion's smiling face to Bob's to Eunice's. "What's this for?"

Bob reached across the table to cover her hand with his. "I guess you could say it's an investment. You've been walking around here for two months looking as though you've lost your last friend, so your mother and I decided you needed a lift. It's enough for the down payment on that old house you wanted, isn't it?"

Amanda swallowed, reading the numbers on the check in disbelief. It was five times the down payment the owner demanded—Amanda still called once a week to see if the house had sold, and had gone to see it twice—and must have represented a major chunk of her parents' savings account. "I can't take this," she said. "You've worked so hard and budgeted so carefully...."

But Bob and Marion presented a united front, and they were backed up by a beaming Eunice, who was now working full-time at the university and living in her own apartment.

"You have to accept it," Marion said firmly. "We won't take no for an answer."

"But suppose I fail?" Since the breakup with Jordan, Amanda's confidence had taken a decided dip, and everything was more difficult than it should have been.

"You won't," Bob said with certainty. "Now call that real estate woman and make an offer before the place is snapped up by some doctor or lawyer looking for a summer house."

Amanda hesitated only a moment. Hope was fluttering in her heart like a bird rising skyward; for the first time in two months she could see herself as a happy woman. With a shriek of delight, she bolted out of her chair and dashed for the telephone, and Bob and Marion laughed until they had tears in their eyes.

The real estate agent was delighted at Amanda's offer, and offered to bring the papers over to Seattle for her to sign. They agreed to meet Monday morning at Amanda's office in the Evergreen Hotel.

When Amanda was off the phone, she turned to her parents. "I can't believe you're doing this for me—taking such a chance—"

"A person can't expect to win in life if they're afraid to take a risk," Bob said quietly.

Amanda went back to the table and bent to hug each of her parents. "You'll be proud of me," she promised.

"We already are," Marion assured her.

On Monday morning Amanda arrived at work with a carefully typed letter of resignation tucked into her briefcase. In another two weeks she would be rolling up her sleeves and making a start on her dream—or, at least, part of it.

She flipped through the messages on her desk, sorting them in order of importance, and at the same time looked into the future. The house she was buying was hardly more than a mile from Jordan's place. She was bound to meet him on the highway or run into him in the supermarket, and she wondered if she could deal with that.

Even after two months Amanda ached every time she thought of Jordan. Actually encountering him face-to-face might really set her back.

There was a rap at the door, and Mindy stepped in, smiling. "You look pretty cheerful today. What's going on? Did you and Jordan get back together or something?"

Amanda opened her briefcase and took out the letter of resignation, keeping her eyes down to hide the sudden pain the mention of Jordan had caused her. "No," she answered, "but I'll be leaving the Evergreen in a couple of weeks— I'm buying that house I wanted on Vashon Island."

"Wow," Mindy responded. "That's great!"

Amanda lifted her eyes to meet her friend's gaze. "Thanks, Mindy."

Mindy's brow puckered in a frown. "I'll miss you a lot, though."

"And I'll miss you." At that moment the inter-com on Amanda's telephone buzzed, and she picked up the receiver as Mindy left the office. "Amanda Scott."

"Ms. Scott, this is Betty Prestwood, Prest-wood Real Estate. I'm afraid I've been delayed, so I won't be arriving in the city until around noon. Could we possibly meet at Ivar's for lunch at twelve-fifteen? I'll have the proper papers with me, of course."

Amanda automatically glanced at her calen-dar, even though she already knew she was free for lunch that day. She probably would have eaten yogurt in her office or gone to the mall with Mindy for fast food. "That will be fine."

After ending that phone call, Amanda went to the executive manager's office suite and handed in her resignation. Mr. Mansfield, a middle-aged man with a bald head and an ulcer, was not pleased that his trusty assistant manager was leaving.

He instructed her to start preliminary interviews for a replacement as soon as possible.

Amanda spent the rest of the morning on the telephone with various employment agencies in the city, and when it came time to meet Mrs. Prestwood for lunch, she was relieved. It wasn't the food that attracted her, but the prospect of a break.

After exchanging her high heels for sneakers, Amanda walked the six blocks from the hotel to the seafood restaurant on the waterfront. The sun was shining, and the harbor was its usual noisy, busy self.

Mrs. Prestwood, a small, trim woman with carefully coiffed blond hair and tasteful makeup, was waiting by the reservations desk.

She and Amanda shook hands, then followed the hostess to a table by a window.

Just as Amanda was sitting down, she spotted Jordan—it was as though her eyes were magnetized to him. He looked very Wall Street in his three-piece suit as he lunched with two other men and a woman.

Evidently he'd sensed Amanda's stare, for his eyes shifted to her almost instantly.

For a moment the whole restaurant seemed to fall into eerie silence for Amanda; she had the odd sensation of standing on the bottom of the ocean. It was only with enormous effort that she surfaced and forced her gaze to the menu the waitress had handed her. *Don't let him come over here,* she prayed silently. *If he does, I'll fall apart right in front of everybody.*

"Is something wrong?" Betty Prestwood asked pleasantly.

Amanda swallowed and shook her head, but out of the corner of her eye she was watching Jordan.

He had turned his attention back to his companions, especially the woman, who was attractive, in a tweedy sort of way, with her trim suit and her dark hair pulled back into a French twist. She was laughing at something Jordan had said.

Amanda made herself study the menu, even though she couldn't have eaten if her life depended on it. She finally decided on the spinach salad and iced tea, just for show.

Mrs. Prestwood brought out the contracts as soon as the waitress had taken their orders, and Amanda read them through carefully. Lunch had arrived by the time she was done, and in a glance she saw that Jordan and his party were leaving. He was resting his hand lightly on the small of the woman's back, and Amanda felt for all the world like a betrayed wife.

Forcing her eyes back to the contracts, she signed them and handed Mrs. Prestwood a check. Since the owner was financing the sale himself, it was now just a matter of waiting for closing. Amanda could rent the house in the interim if she wished.

She wrote another check, then stabbed a leaf of spinach with her fork. Try as she might, she couldn't lift it to her mouth. Her stomach was roiling angrily, unwilling to accept anything.

She laid the fork down.

"Is everything all right?" Mrs. Prestwood asked, seeming genuinely concerned.

Amanda lied by nodding her head.

"You don't seem very hungry."

Amanda managed a smile. Was Jordan sleeping with that woman? Did she visit him on the island on weekends? "I'm just getting over the flu," she said, which was at least a partial truth. She was probably coming down with it, not getting over it.

Mrs. Prestwood accepted that excuse and finished her lunch in good time. The two women parted outside the restaurant with another handshake, then Amanda started back up the hill to the hotel. By the time she arrived, her head was pounding and there were two people waiting to be interviewed for her job.

She talked to both of them and didn't pass either application on to Mr. Mansfield for his consideration. One had obviously considered herself too good for such a menial position, and the other had an offensive personal manner.

Amanda's headache got progressively worse as the afternoon passed, but she was too busy interviewing to go home to bed, and besides, she couldn't be sure the malady wasn't psychosomatic. She hadn't started feeling really sick until after she'd seen Jordan with that woman in the dress-for-success clothes.

At the end of the day Amanda dragged herself home, fed Gershwin, made herself a bowl of chicken noodle soup and watched the evening news in her favorite bathrobe. By the time she'd been apprised of all the shootings, rapes, drug deals and political scandals of the day, she was thoroughly depressed. She put her empty soup bowl in the sink, took two aspirin and fell into bed.

The next morning she felt really terrible. Her head seemed thick and heavy as a medicine ball, and her chest ached.

Reluctantly she called in sick, took more aspirin and went back to sleep.

A loud knocking at the door awakened her around eleven-thirty, and Amanda rolled out of bed, stumbled into the living room with one hand pressed to her aching head and called, "Who is it?"

"It's me," a feminine voice replied. "Mindy. Let me in—I come bearing gifts."

With a sigh, Amanda undid the chains, twisted the lock and opened the door. "You're taking your life in your hands, coming in here," she warned in a thick voice. "This place is infested with germs."

Mindy's pretty hair was sprinkled with raindrops, and her smile was warm. "I'll risk it," she said, stepping past Amanda with a stack of magazines and a box of something that smelled good. She grimaced as she assessed Amanda's rumpled nightgown and unbrushed hair. "You look like the victim in a horror movie," she observed cheerfully. "Sit down before you fall down."

Amanda dropped into a chair. "What's going on at the office?"

"It's bedlam," Mindy answered, setting the magazines and food down on the table to shrug out of her coat. "Mr. Mansfield is finding out just how valuable you really are." Her voice trailed back from the kitchenette, where she was opening cupboards and drawers. "He's been interviewing all morning, and he's such a bear today, he'll be lucky if anybody wants to work for him."

Amanda sighed. "I should be there."

Mindy returned from the kitchenette and handed Amanda a plate of the fried Chinese noodles she knew she loved. "And spread bubonic plague among your friends and co-workers? Bad idea. Eat this, Amanda."

Amanda took the plate of noodles and dug in with a fork. Although she still had no appetite, she knew her body needed food to recover, and she hadn't had anything to eat since last night's chicken soup. "Thanks."

Mindy glanced at the blank TV screen in amazement. "Do you mean to tell me you have a chance to catch up on all the soaps and you aren't even watching?"

"I'm sick, not on vacation," Amanda pointed out.

Mindy rushed to turn on the set and tune in her favorite. "Lord, will you look at him?" she asked, pointing to a shirtless hero soulfully telling a woman she was the only one for him.

"Don't listen to him," Amanda muttered. "As soon as you make one wrong move, he'll dump you."

"You *have* been watching this show!" Mindy accused.

Amanda shook her head glumly. "I was speaking from the perspective of real life," she said, chewing.

Mindy sighed. "I knew that rascal would be fooling around with Lorinda the minute Jennifer turned her back," she fretted, shaking her finger at the screen.

Amanda chuckled, even though she would have had to feel better just to die, and took another bite of the noodles Mindy had brought. "How do you know so much about the story line when you work every day?"

"I tape it," Mindy answered. Then, somewhat reluctantly, she snapped off the set and turned back to her mission of mercy. "Is there anything you want me to do at the office, Amanda? Or I could shop for you—"

Amanda interrupted with a shake of her head. "It's enough that you came over. That was really nice of you."

Mindy rose from the couch and put her hands on her slim hips. "I know. I'll make a bed for you on the couch so you can watch TV. Mom always did that for me when I was sick, and it never failed to cheer me up."

With that, Mindy disappeared into the bedroom, returning soon afterward with sheets, blankets and pillows. True to her word, she made a place for Amanda on the couch and all but tucked her in when she was settled with her magazines and the controls for the TV.

Before going back to work, she made Amanda a cup of hot tea, put the phone within reach and forced her to take more aspirin.

When Mindy was gone, Amanda got up to lock the door behind her, then padded back to the bed. She was comfortably settled when the telephone rang. A queer feeling quivered in the pit of her stomach as she remembered seeing Jordan in the restaurant the day before, felt again the electricity that passed between them when their eyes met. "Hello?" she said hopefully.

"Hello, Amanda."

The voice didn't belong to Jordan, but to Mrs. Prestwood. Amanda could pick up the keys to her house at the real estate office whenever she was ready.

Amanda promised to be there within the week, and asked Mrs. Prestwood to have telephone service hooked up at the house, along with electricity. Then she hung up and flipped slowly through the magazines, seeing none of the glossy photographs and enticing article titles. She was going to be living on the same island with Jordan, and that was all she could think about.

By the time Amanda recovered enough to return to work, half her notice was up and Mr. Mansfield had selected a replacement. Handing her her final paycheck, which was sizable because there was vacation pay added in, he wished her well. On her last day, he and Mindy and the others held a going away party for her in the hotel's elegant lounge, and Bob, Marion and Eunice attended, too.

That Friday evening, Amanda filled her car with boxes, one of which contained Gershwin, leaving the rest of her things behind for the movers to bring, and boarded the ferry for Vashon Island.

Since it was cold and dark in the bottom of the ship, she decided to venture upstairs to the snack bar for a cup of hot coffee. Just as she arrived, however, she spotted Jordan again. This time he was with his daughters, and the three of them were eating French fries while both girls talked at once.

Amanda's first instinct was to approach them and say hello, but in the end she lost her courage and slipped back out of the snack bar and down the stairs to her car. She sat hunched behind the wheel, waiting for the whistle announcing their arrival at Vashon Island to blast, and feeling miserable. What kind of life was she going to have in her new community if she had to worry about avoiding Jordan?

In those moments Amanda felt terribly alone, and the enormity of the things she'd done—giving up her job and apartment and borrowing such a staggering sum of money from her parents—oppressed her.

Finally the ferry came into port, and Amanda drove her car down the ramp, wondering if Jordan and the girls were in one of the cars ahead, or one behind. She didn't get a glimpse of them, which wasn't surprising, considering how dark it was.

When Amanda arrived at her new old house, the lights were on and Mrs. Prestwood was waiting in the kitchen to present the key, since Amanda had not had a chance to pick it up at the office. The old oil furnace was rumbling beneath the floor, filling the spacious rooms with warmth.

Amanda wandered through the rooms, sipping coffee from the percolator Betty Prestwood had thoughtfully loaned her and dreaming of the things she meant to do. There would be winter parties around the huge fireplace in the front parlor—she would serve mulled wine and spice cake with whipped cream. And in summer, guests could sleep on the screened sun porch if they wanted to, and be lulled into slumber by the quiet rhythm of the tide and the salty whisper of the breezes.

There were seven bedrooms upstairs, but only one bathroom. Amanda made a mental note to call in a plumbing contractor for estimates the next morning. She would have to add at least one more.

Amanda's private room, a small one off the kitchen, looked especially inviting after the long day she'd had. While Gershwin continued to explore the farthest reaches of his new home, she went out to the car to get the cot and sleeping bag she'd borrowed from her stepdad. After a bath upstairs, she crawled onto the cot with a book.

She hadn't read more than a page, when Gershwin suddenly landed in the middle of her stomach with a plop and meow.

Amanda let her book rest against her chin and stroked his silky fur. "Don't worry, Big Guy. We're both going to like it here." The instant the words were out of her mouth, though, she thought of the jolt that seeing Jordan and the girls had caused her, and her throat tightened painfully. "You'd think I'd be over him by now, wouldn't you?" she said when she could speak, her vision so blurred that there seemed to be two Gershwins lying on her stomach instead of one.

"Reoww," Gershwin agreed, before bending his head to lick one of his paws.

"Love is hell," Amanda went on with a sniffle. "Be glad you're neutered."

Gershwin made no comment on that, so Amanda dried her eyes and focused determinedly on her book again.

The next morning brought a storm in off Puget Sound. It slashed at the windows and howled around the corners of the house, and Gershwin kept himself within six inches of Amanda's feet. She left him only to carry in the boxes from the car and drive to the supermarket for food.

Since she'd prepared herself to encounter Jordan, Amanda was both relieved and disappointed when there was no sign of him. She filled her cart with groceries, taking care to buy a can of Gershwin's favorite food to make up for leaving him, and drove back over rain-slickened roads to the house.

The tempest raged all day, but Amanda was fascinated by it, rather than frightened. While Gershwin was sleeping off the feast Amanda had brought him, she put on her slicker and a pair of rubber boots she'd found in the basement and walked down to the beach.

Lightning cracked the sky like a mirror dropped on a hard floor, and the water lashed furiously at the rocky shoreline. Amanda stood with her hands in the pockets of her slicker, watching the spectacle in awe.

When she returned to the house half an hour later, her jeans were wet to her knees despite the rain garb she wore, and her hair was dripping. She felt strangely comforted, though, and when she saw Betty Prestwood's car splashing up the puddle-riddled driveway, she smiled and waved.

The two women dashed onto the enclosed porch together, laughing. Betty was only a few years older than Amanda, and they were getting to be good friends.

"There's an estate sale scheduled for today," Betty said breathlessly when they were in the kitchen and Amanda had handed her a cup of steaming coffee. "I thought you might like to go, since you need so much furniture. It's just on the other side of the island, and we could have lunch out."

Amanda was pleased that Betty had thought of her. Even though she had a surplus of funds, thanks to her own savings and the loan from Bob and Marion, it was going to cost a lot of money to get the bed and breakfast into operation. She needed to furnish the place attractively for a reasonable price. "Sounds great," Amanda said, ruefully comparing her soggy jeans and crumpled flannel shirt to Betty's stylish pink suit. "Just give me a few minutes, and I'll change."

Betty smiled. "Fine. Do you mind if I use the phone? I like to check in with the office periodically."

Amanda gestured toward the wall phone between the sink and stove. "Help yourself. And have some more coffee if you want it. I won't be long."

After finding a pair of black woolen slacks and a burgundy sweater, along with clean underthings and a towel and washcloth, Amanda dashed upstairs and took a quick, hot shower. When she was dressed, with her hair blow-dried and a light application of makeup highlighting her features, she hurried downstairs.

Betty was leaning against one of the kitchen counters, sipping coffee. "When are the movers coming?"

"Monday," Amanda answered, pulling on a pair of shoes that would probably be ruined the instant she wore them outside. "But even when all my stuff is here, the place is still going to echo like a cavern."

Betty laughed. "Maybe we can fix that this afternoon."

After saying goodbye to Gershwin, who still hadn't recovered from his stupor, Amanda pulled the ugly rubber boots she'd worn earlier on over her shoes, put on her slicker and followed Betty to her car.

Since the auction was scheduled for one o'clock, they had time for a leisurely lunch. Mercifully Betty suggested a small soup-and-sandwich place in town, rather than the roadside café Amanda knew Jordan frequented.

She ordered a turkey sandwich with bean sprouts, along with a bowl of minestrone, and ate with enthusiasm. She wasn't over Jordan, and she was still weak with lingering traces of the flu, but her appetite was back.

After lunch, she and Betty drove to a secluded house on the opposite side of the island, where folding chairs had been set up under huge pink-and-white striped canopies. Amanda's heart sank when she saw how many people had braved the nasty weather in search of a bargain, but Betty seemed to be taking a positive attitude, so she tried to follow suit.

The articles available for sale were scattered throughout the house—there were pianos and bedroom sets, tea services and bureaus, sets of china boasting imprints like Limoges and Haviland. Embroidered linens were offered, too, along with exquisite lace curtains and grandfather clocks, and wonderful old books that smelled of age and refinement.

Amanda's excitement built, and she crossed her fingers as she and Betty took their places in the horde of metal chairs.

A beautiful old sleigh bed with a matching bureau and armoire came up for sale first, and Amanda, thinking of her seven empty bedrooms, held up her bid card when the auctioneer asked for a modest amount to start the sale rolling.

A man in the back row bid against her, and it was nip and tuck, but Amanda finally won the skirmish with fairly minimal damage to her bank balance.

After that she bought linens, one of the grandfather clocks and a set of English bone china, while Betty purchased a full-length mirror in a cherrywood stand and an old jewelry box. At the end of the sale, Amanda made arrangements for the auction company to deliver her purchases, then wrote out a check.

It was midafternoon by then, and her soup and sandwich were beginning to wear off. Having lost sight of Betty in the crowd, she bought a hot dog with mustard and relish and a diet cola, then sat quietly in one of the folding chairs to eat.

She nearly choked when Jordan walked up, turned the chair in front of hers around and straddled it, his arms draped across the back. His expression was every bit as remote as it had been the last time she'd seen him, and Amanda prayed he couldn't hear her heart thudding against her rib cage.

"What are you doing here?" he asked, his voice insinuating that she was probably up to no good.

Amanda was instantly offended. She swallowed a chunk of her hot dog in a painful lump and replied, "I thought I'd try to steal some of the silverware, or maybe palm an antique broach or two."

He grinned, though the expression didn't quite reach his eyes. "You bought a bedroom set, a grandfather clock and some dishes. Getting married, Ms. Scott, now that Mrs. Brockman is out of the picture?"

It was all Amanda could do not to poke him in the eye with the rest of her hot dog. Obviously he didn't know she'd bought the Victorian house, and she wasn't about to tell him. "It'll be a June wedding," she said evenly. "Would you like to come?"

"I'm busy for the rest of the decade," Jordan answered in a taut voice, his hazel eyes snapping as he rose from the chair and put it back into line with the others. "See you around."

As abruptly as that, he was gone, and Amanda was left to sit there wondering why she'd let him walk away. When Betty returned, bringing along two of her friends to be introduced, Amanda was staring glumly at her unfinished hot dog.

Because Jessie and Lisa were staying with Becky's parents in Bellevue that weekend, Jordan was driving the Porsche. He strode back to it, oblivious to the rain saturating his hair and his shirt, and threw himself behind the wheel, slamming the door behind him.

Damn it all to hell, if Amanda was going to go on as if nothing had happened between them, couldn't she at least stay on her own turf? It drove him crazy, catching glimpses of her in restaurants, and in the midst of crowds waiting to cross streets, and in the next aisle at bookstores.

After slamming his palms against the steering wheel once, he turned the key in the ignition, and the powerful engine surged to life. The decision had been made by the time the conglomeration of striped canopies had disappeared from the rear-view mirror; he would go home, change his clothes and spend the rest of the day in Seattle, working.

The plan seemed to be falling into place until an hour later, when he was passing by that Victorian place Amanda had liked so much. The lights were on, and there was a familiar car parked in the driveway.

He met Betty Prestwood's pink Cadillac midway between the highway and the house. She smiled and waved, and Jordan waved back distractedly, noticing for the first time that the For Sale sign was gone from the yard.

He braked the car to a stop and sprinted through the rain to the door, feeling a peculiar mixture of elation and outrage as he hammered at it with one fist.

# 11

Amanda had just changed back into her jeans and a T-shirt when the thunderous knock sounded at the door. Expecting an enthusiastic salesperson, she was taken aback to find Jordan standing on her porch, dripping rainwater and indignation.

"Aren't you going to ask me in?" he demanded.

Amanda stepped back without a word, watching with round eyes as Jordan stomped into the warm kitchen, scowling at her.

"Well?" he prompted, putting his hands on his hips.

He seemed to have a particular scenario in mind, but Amanda couldn't think for the life of her what it would be.

She left him standing there while she went into her bathroom for a dry towel. Handing it to him upon her return, she asked, "Well, what?"

"What are you doing in this house? For that matter, what are you doing on this *island*?" He was drying his hair all the while he spoke, a grudging expression on his face.

Amanda hooked her thumbs in the waistband of her jeans and tilted her head to one side. "I own this house," she replied. "As for why I'm on the island, well—" she paused to shrug and spread her hands "—I guess I just didn't know I was supposed to get your approval before I stepped off the ferry."

Jordan flung the towel across the room, and it caught on the handle of the old-fashioned refrigerator. "Are you married to James?"

She went to the percolator and filled two cups with coffee, one for her and one for Jordan. "No," she answered, turning her head to look back at him over her shoulder. "I explained the situation to you. I was only trying to help James in my own misguided way. Where did you get the idea I meant to marry him?"

Jordan sighed and shoved his hand through damp, tangled hair. "Okay, so my imagination ran away with me. I tried to call you on Christmas Eve, and you weren't home. I had all these pictures in my mind of you lying on some secluded beach in Hawaii, helping James recuperate."

Although she was delighted, even jubilant, to know Jordan had tried to call her, she wasn't about to let on. She brought the coffee cup to him and held it out until he took it. "How would my lying on a secluded beach help James recuperate?"

"With you for a visual aid, a corpse would recuperate," he replied with a sheepish grin. His eyes remained serious. "I've missed you, Mandy."

She felt tears rising in her eyes and lowered her head while she struggled to hold them back. She didn't trust herself to speak.

Jordan took her coffee and set it, with his own, on the counter. "Don't you have any chairs in this place?"

Amanda made herself meet his eyes as she shook her head. "Not yet. The movers will be here on Monday."

He approached her, hooked his index fingers through the belt loops on her jeans and pulled her close. So close that every intimacy they'd ever shared came surging back to her memory at the contact, making her feel light-headed.

"I may have neglected to mention this before," he said in a voice like summer thunder rumbling far in the distance, "but I'm in love with you, and I have a feeling it's a lifetime thing."

Amanda linked her hands behind his neck, reveling in her closeness to Jordan and the priceless words he'd just said. "Actually, you did neglect to mention that, Mr. Richards."

He tasted her lips, sending a thrill careening through her system. "I apologize abjectly, even though you're guilty of the same oversight."

"Only too true," Amanda whispered, her mouth against his. "I love you, Jordan."

He ran his hands up and down her back, strong and sure and full of the power to set her senses aflame. He pressed his lips to her neck and answered with a teasing growl.

Amanda called upon all her self-control to lean back in his arms. "Jordan, we have things to talk about—things to work out. We can't just take up where we left off."

His fingers were hooked in her belt loops again. "I'll grant you that we have a lot to work through, and it's going to take some time. Why don't we go over to my place and talk?"

With considerable effort, Amanda willed her heart to slow down to a normal beat. She knew what was going to happen—it was inevitable—but she wanted to be sure they were on solid ground first. "We can talk here," she said, and she led him into the giant, empty parlor with its view of the sound. They sat together on a window seat with no cushion, their hands clasped. "I was wrong not to tell you I was seeing James again, Jordan, and I'm sorry."

He touched her lips with an index finger. Outside, beyond the rain-dappled glass, the storm raged on. "Looking back, I guess I wouldn't have been very receptive, anyway. I was feeling pretty possessive."

Amanda rested her head against his damp shoulder, unable to resist his warmth any longer, trembling as he traced a tingling pattern on her nape. "I thought I was going to die when I saw you at Ivar's with that corporation chick."

Jordan laughed and curved his fingers under her chin. "'Corporation chick'? That was Clarissa Robbins. She works in the legal department and is married to one of my best friends."

Amanda felt foolish, but she was also relieved, and she guessed that showed in her face, because Jordan was grinning at her. "You have your girls back," she said. "I saw you on the ferry last night."

Jordan nodded. "They didn't actually move in until a month ago. After all, they were used to living with Paul and Karen, so we just did weekends at first. And they're staying with Becky's parents until tomorrow night."

She tried to lower her head again, but Jordan wouldn't allow it.

"Think you could fall for a guy with two kids, Mandy?" he asked.

"I already have," she answered softly.

Jordan's mouth descended to hers, gentle at first, and then possessive and commanding. By the time he withdrew, Amanda was dazed.

"Show me the bridal suite," he said, rising to his feet and pulling Amanda after him.

She swallowed. "There's no bed in there, Jordan," she explained timidly.

"Where do you sleep?"

His voice was downright hypnotic. In fact, if he'd started undressing her right there in the middle of the parlor, she wouldn't have been able to raise an objection. "In a little room off the kitchen, but—"

"Show me," Jordan interrupted, and she led him back to where she slept.

"That'll never hold up," he said, eyeing the cot Amanda had spent the night on. With an inspired grin, he grabbed up the sleeping bag and pillow. "Now," he went on, grasping her hand again, "let's break in the bridal suite."

Amanda felt color rise in her cheeks, and she averted her eyes before leading the way around to the front of the house and up the stairs.

The best room faced the water and boasted its own fireplace, but it was unfurnished except for a large hooked rug centered in the middle of the floor.

Jordan spread the sleeping bag out on the rug and tossed the pillow carelessly on top of it, then stood watching Amanda with a mingling of humor and hunger in his eyes. "Come here, Mandy," he said with gentle authority.

She approached him shyly, because in some ways everything was new between them.

He slipped his hands beneath her T-shirt, resting them lightly on the sides of her waist; his hands were surprisingly warm.

"I love you, Amanda Scott," he told her firmly. "And in a month or a year or whenever you're ready, I'm going to make you my wife. Any objections?"

Amanda's lips were dry, and she wet them with her tongue. "None at all," she answered, and she drew in a sharp breath and closed her eyes as Jordan slid his hands up her sides to her breasts. With his thumbs he stroked her long-neglected nipples through the lacy fabric of her bra. When they stood erect, he pulled Amanda's T-shirt off over her head and tossed it aside.

"Let me look at you," he said, standing back a little.

Slowly, a little awkwardly, Amanda unhooked her bra and let it drop, revealing her full breasts. She let her hand fall back in ecstatic surrender as Jordan boldly closed his hands over her. When he bent his head and began to suckle at one pulsing nipple, she gave a little cry and entangled her hands in his hair.

He drew on both her breasts, one after the other, until she was half-delirious, and then he dropped to his knees on the sleeping bag and gently took Amanda's shoes from her feet. She started to sink down, needing union with him, but he grasped her hips and held her upright.

She bit down on her lower lip as she felt his finger beneath the waistband of her jeans. The snap gave way, and then the zipper, and then Amanda was bared to him, except for her panties and socks.

Her knees bent of their own accord, and her pelvis shifted forward as Jordan nipped at the hidden mound, all the time rolling one of her socks down. When her feet were bare, he pulled her panties down very slowly, and she kicked them aside impatiently, sure that Jordan would appease her now.

But he wasn't through tormenting her. He massaged the insides of her thighs, carefully avoiding the place that most needed his attention, and then lifted one of her knees and placed it over his shoulder.

Amanda was forced to link her hands behind his neck to keep from falling. "Oh," she whimpered as she realized what a vulnerable position she was in. "Jordan—"

He parted her with his fingers. "What?"

Her answer was cut off, and forced forever into the recesses of her mind when Jordan suddenly took her fully, greedily, into his mouth. She thrust her head back with the proud abandon of a tigress and gave a primitive groan that echoed in the empty room.

Jordan raised one hand to fondle her breast as he consumed her, and the two sensations combined to drive her to the very edge of sanity. She began to plead with him, and tug at the back of his shirt in a fruitless effort to strip him and feel his nakedness under her hands.

He lay back on the floor, bringing Amanda with him, and she rocked wildly in a shameless search for release while he moved his hands in gentle circles on her quivering belly. When he caught both her nipples between his fingers, Amanda's quest ended in a spectacular explosion that wrung a series of hoarse cries from her throat.

She sagged to the floor when it was over, only half-conscious, and Jordan arranged her on the sleeping bag before slowly removing his clothes. When he was naked, he tucked the pillow under her bottom and parted her knees, kneeling between them to tease her.

The back of one hand resting against her mouth, Amanda gave a soft moan. "Jordan—"

"Umm?" He gave her barely an inch of himself, but that was enough to arouse her all over again, to stir the fires he'd just banked. At the same time, he bent to sip at one of her nipples in a leisurely fashion.

Amanda groaned.

"What was that?" Jordan teased, barely pausing in his enjoyment of her breast.

"I want—oh, God, Jordan, please—I need you so much...."

He drew in a ragged breath, and she felt him tremble against the insides of her thighs as he gave her another inch.

She clutched at his arms, trying to pull him to her. "Jordan!" she wailed suddenly in utter desperation, and he gave her just a little more of himself.

Amanda couldn't wait any longer. She'd had release once, it was true, but her every instinct drove her toward complete fulfillment. She needed Jordan's weight, his substance, his force, and she needed it immediately.

With a fierce cry, she thrust her hips upward, taking him all the way inside her, and at that point Jordan's awesome control snapped.

Amanda watched through a haze of passion as he surrendered. Bracing his hands on the rug and arching his back, he withdrew and lunged into her again in a long, violent stroke, leaving no doubt as to the extent of his claim on her.

Triumph came at the peak of a sweet frenzy that tore a rasping shout from Jordan's throat and set Amanda's spirit to spiraling within her. For a few dizzying moments she was sure it would escape and soar off into the cosmos, leaving her body behind forever. The feeling passed, like a fever, and when Jordan fell to her, she was there to receive him.

He kissed her bare shoulder between gasps for air, and finally whispered, "Don't mind me. I'll be fine in a year or two."

Amanda's breath had just returned, and she laughed, moving her hands over his back in a gesture meant both to soothe and to claim. But her eyes were solemn when Jordan lifted his head to study her face a few moments later.

"Do you think it will take a long time for us to get things ironed out, Jordan?"

He kissed her forehead. "Judging by what just happened here, I'd say no."

"Good," she answered.

He traced the outline of her mouth with the tip of one finger. "Will you give me a baby, Mandy?" he asked huskily.

Her heart warmed within her, and seemed to grow larger. "Probably sooner than you think," she replied.

Jordan chuckled and drew her close to him, and they lay together for a long time, recovering. Remembering. Finally, he bent to kiss her once more before rising from her to reach for his clothes. He gave her a long look as she sat up and wrapped her arms around her knees, then sighed. "We've got a lot of talking to do," he said. "Now that there's some chance of concentrating, let's go over to my place and get started."

Amanda nodded and grabbed her jeans and panties. Because her things were scattered all over the rug, she wasn't able to dress as fast as Jordan, and he was brazen enough to watch her put on every garment.

Fifteen minutes later they pulled into his garage. When a blaze was snapping in the living room fireplace, they sat side by side on the floor in front of it, cross-legged and sipping wine.

Amanda started the conversation with a blunt but necessary question. "Are you still in love with Becky?"

Jordan considered her words solemnly and for a long time. "Not in the way you mean," he finally said, his eyes caressing Amanda he watched her reactions. "But I'll always care about her. It's just that I feel a different kind of love for her now. Sort of mellow and quiet and nostalgic."

Amanda nodded, then let her head rest against his shoulder. "In a way, she lives on in Jessie and Lisa."

Jordan sighed, watching the fire. He told her about the accident then, about feeling Becky's arms tighten around his waist in fear just before impact, about the pain, about being in the hospital when her funeral was held. "I felt responsible for her death for a long time," he said, "but I finally realized I was just using that as an excuse to go on mourning forever. Deep down inside, I knew it was really an accident."

Amanda gave him a hug.

"Thanks, Mandy," he said hoarsely.

She sat up straight to look at him. "For what?"

"For coming along when you did, and for being who you are. Until I met you, I didn't think love was an option for me."

The rain began to slacken in its seemingly incessant chatter on the roof and against the windows, and Amanda thought she saw a hint of sunshine glimmering at the edge of a distant cloud.

She linked her arm through Jordan's and laid her temple to his shoulder, content just to be close to him.

Jordan intertwined his fingers with Amanda's, and his grip was strong and tight. With his other hand he tapped his wineglass against hers. "Here's to taking chances," he said softly.

The movers arrived on Monday, and so did the furniture Amanda had bought at the estate sale. She called in several plumbers for estimates on extra bathrooms, and that night she and Jordan and the girls sat around her kitchen table, eating chicken from a red-and-white striped bucket.

"I'm glad you didn't go to heaven," Jessie told Amanda, her dark eyes round and earnest.

"Me, too," Lisa put in, nibbling on a drumstick.

Amanda's gaze linked with Jordan's. "I could have sworn I visited there once," she said mysteriously.

Jordan gave her a look. "Dirty pool, lady," he accused.

"Uh-uh, Daddy," Jessie argued. "Amanda doesn't even *have* a pool."

"I stand corrected," Jordan told his daughter, but his eyes were on Amanda.

Tossing a denuded chicken bone onto her plate, Amanda stood up and bent to give greasy, top-of-the-head kisses to both Jessie and Lisa. "Thanks for being glad I'm around, gang," she told the girls in a conspiratorial whisper.

"You're welcome," Jessie replied.

Lisa was busy tilting the bucket to see if there was another drumstick inside.

Jordan watched Amanda with mischievous eyes as she dropped her plate into the trash and then leaned back against the sink with her arms folded.

"I suppose you people think I can't cook," she said.

No one offered a comment except for Gershwin, who came strolling into the kitchen with a cordial meow. The girls were delighted, and instantly abandoned what remained of their dinners to pet him.

When he realized he wasn't going to get any chicken, the cat wandered out of the room again. Jessie and Lisa were right behind him.

"Come here," Jordan said with just the hint of a grin.

"I've got no willpower at all where you're concerned," Amanda answered, allowing herself to be pulled onto his lap.

"Good. Will you marry me, Mandy?"

She tilted her head to one side. "Yes. But we agreed to wait, give things time—"

"We've had enough time. I love you, and that's never going to change."

Amanda kissed him. "If it's never going to change, then it won't matter if we wait."

He let his forehead fall against her breasts, pretending to be forlorn. "Do you know what it's going to do to me to go home tonight and leave you here?" he muttered.

She rested her chin on the top of his head. "You'll survive," she assured him. "I need a few months to get the business going, Jordan."

He sighed heavily. "Okay," he said with such a tone of martyrdom that Amanda laughed out loud.

Jordan repaid her by sliding a hand up under her shirt and cupping her breast.

Amanda squirmed and uttered a protest, but the steady strokes of his thumb across her nipple raised a fever in her. "We'll just have to be—flexible," she acquiesced with a sigh of supreme longing.

"We're not going to have much time alone together," Jordan warned, continuing his quiet campaign to drive her crazy. "Of course, if we were married, it would be perfectly natural for us to sleep together every night." He'd lifted one side of Amanda's bra so that her bare breast nestled in his hand.

"Jordan," Amanda whispered. "Stop it."

In the parlor, Amanda's television set came on, and the theme song of the girls' favorite sitcom filled the air. "A nuclear war wouldn't distract them from that show," Jordan said sleepily, lifting Amanda's T-shirt and closing his lips brazenly around her nipple.

She knew she should twist away, but the truth was, the most she could manage was to turn on Jordan's lap so that she could see the parlor doorway clearly. The position provided Jordan with better access to her breast, which he enjoyed without a hint of self-consciousness.

When he'd had enough, he righted her bra, pulled her shirt down and swatted her lightly on the bottom. "Well," he said with an exaggerated yawn, "it's a school night. I'd better take the girls home."

Amanda was indignant. "Jordan Richards, you deliberately got me worked up...."

He grinned and lifted her off his lap. "Yep," he confessed, rising from his chair and wandering idly in the direction of the parlor.

Flushed, Amanda flounced back and forth between the table and the trash can, disposing of the remains of dinner. After that, she wiped the table off in furious motions, and when she carried the dishcloth back to the sink, she realized Jordan was watching her with a twinkle in his eyes.

"In three days we could have a license," he said.

In the parlor, Jessie and Lisa laughed at some event in their favorite program, and the sound lifted Amanda's heart. The children would always be Becky and Jordan's, but she loved them already, and she wanted to be a part of their lives almost as much as she wanted to be a part of their father's.

She walked slowly over to the man she loved and put her arms around his waist. "Okay, Jordan, you win. I want to be with you and the kids too much to wait any longer. But you'll have to be patient with me, because getting a new business off the ground takes a lot of time and energy."

His eyes danced with delight as he lifted one hand for a solemn oath. "I'll be patient if you will," he said.

Amanda bit down on her lower lip, worried. "I don't want to fail at this, Jordan."

He kissed her forehead. "We'll have to work at marriage, Mandy—just like everybody else does. But it'll last, I promise you."

"How can you be so sure?" she asked, watching his face for some sign of reservation or caution.

She saw only confidence and love. "The odds are in our favor," he answered, "and I'm taking the rest on faith."

It was September, and the maples and elms scattered between the evergreens across the road were turning to bright gold. They matched the lumbering yellow school bus that ground to a halt beside the sign that read Amanda's Place.

The bus door opened and Jessie bounded down the steps and leaped to the ground, then turned to catch hold of Lisa's hand and patiently help her down.

Amanda smiled and placed one hand on her distended stomach, watching as her stepdaughters raced toward the house, their school papers fluttering in the autumn breeze.

"I made a house!" Lisa shouted, breathless with excitement as she raced ahead of her sister to meet Amanda on the step.

Amanda bent to properly examine the drawing Lisa had done in the afternoon kindergarten session. A crude square with windows represented the house, and there were four stick figures in front. "Here's me," Lisa said with a sniffle, pointing a pudgy little finger at the smallest form in the picture, "and here's Jessie and Daddy and you. I didn't draw the baby 'cause I don't know what he looks like.''

Amanda kissed the child soundly on the forehead. "That's such a good picture that I'm going to put it up in the shop so everybody who comes in can admire it."

Lisa beamed at the prospect, sniffled again and toddled past Amanda and into the warm kitchen.

"How about you?" she asked Jessie, who had waited patiently on the bottom step for her turn. "Did you draw a picture, too?"

"I'm too big for that," Jessie said importantly. "I wrote the whole alphabet."

Putting an arm on the little girl's back, Amanda gently steered her into the kitchen. "Let's see," she said.

Jessie proudly extended the paper. "I already know enough to be in second grade," she said.

Amanda assessed the neatly printed letters marching smartly across Jessie's paper. "This is certainly one of the nicest papers I've ever seen," she said.

Jessie eyed her shrewdly. "Good enough to be in the shop like Lisa's picture?"

"Absolutely," Amanda replied. To prove her assertion, she strode through the big dining room, now completely furnished, and the large parlor, where Lisa was plunking on the piano, into the shop. Several of her quilts were displayed there, along with the work of many local craftspeople.

Her live-in manager, Millie Delano, was behind the cash register. It had been a slow day, but there were guests scheduled for the weekend, and the quilts and other items had sold extremely well over the summer. Amanda was making a go of her bed and breakfast, although it would be a long time before she got rich.

She held up both Lisa's picture and Jessie's printing for Millie's inspection. The pleasant middle-aged woman smiled broadly as Amanda made places for the papers on the bulletin board behind the counter and pinned them into place.

Jessie, who sometimes worried that her fondness for Amanda made her disloyal to her mother, beamed with pride.

The girls were settled in the kitchen, drinking milk and eating bananas, when Jordan arrived from the city. "Is my family ready to go home?" he asked, poking his head around the door.

Jessie and Lisa, who were always delighted to see him, whether he'd been away five minutes, five hours or five days, flung themselves at him with shrieks of welcome. Amanda, her hands resting on her protruding stomach, stood back, watching. Her eyes brimmed with tears as she thought how lucky she was to have the three of them filling her life with love and confusion and laughter.

After gently freeing himself from his daughters, Jordan walked over to Amanda and laid his hands on either side of her face. With his thumbs he brushed away her tears. "Hi, pregnant lady," he said. A quiet pride made Amanda's heart swell. "Hi," she replied with a soft smile.

He gave her a leisurely kiss, then steered her toward the door. Her coat was hanging on a wooden peg nearby, and he helped her into it before handing Jessie and Lisa their jackets.

Amanda was struck again by the depth of her love for him when, in his tailored suit, he dropped to one knee to help Lisa with a jammed zipper. She couldn't have asked for a better father for her child than Jordan Richards.

When the hectic family project of preparing dinner was behind them, and Lisa and Jessie had had their baths, their stories and their good-night kisses, Jordan led Amanda into the living room. They sat on the sofa in front of a snapping fire, with their heads touching.

Jordan brought his hand to rest on Amanda's stomach, and when the baby kicked, his eyes were as bright as the flames on the hearth. Amanda couldn't help smiling.

He smoothed back a lock of her hair. "Tired?" he asked.

"Yes." Amanda sighed. "How about you?"

"Beat," Jordan replied. "Personally, I don't see that we have any choice but to go straight to bed."

Amanda laughed and thrust herself off the couch. "Last one there is a rotten egg!" she cried, waddling toward the stairs.